FLOOD

ELDON CROWE

Tellwell Talent
www.tellwell.ca

ISBN
978-0-2288-7378-5 (Paperback)

For Lynda, Dean, and Laura.
Love you always.

I

He paced along the River restlessly, yet knew in Truth that he should not.

Danger. The World is dangerous. The Plain. The Land of Elah-Makah. Even…..beyond. In the Grey Mountains.

He shuddered, clutching his bow in his roughened hand.

Yet all of that is out there. NOT in here. How can there be danger within the Valley?

He halted, looking out across the River and saw the might in its rushing waters, its foaming crests, sensed the strength within its bed of rock. He raised his right hand with his bow toward it despite the tightening knot in his gut and forced himself to breathe more deeply. "You know why the River comes," he whispered fiercely, "You know Who sends it here to us in the Valley, Who nourishes and builds up the Land of Seth, the Great Father." He swallowed. *It is what she taught me. She and many others besides. Father. Even the Ancient.*

He spoke all of this aloud to himself as if it were a chant and could ward off the sense of doom that he had felt since dawn. Turning, he cast a quick glance over his shoulder at her but she had not moved a span, remaining crouched beside the rushing waters, her ochre-coloured hood up over her head, her hands yet raised towards the Sky.

Grumbling, he began to pace again, stepping over moss-covered stones, glistening wetly in the low, rising sun that was just peeking over the crowns of the highest trees upon the Valley's Eastern edge. He dared not interrupt her at Prayer, that Sacred Rite to which she gave herself every morning. Yet…..

…..something was not right this morning - even within the Valley - and everything that was usual and normal felt threatened somehow. He could *feel* it. Why could she not? Where were the Birds, the Animals? Why was the Valley so silent?

At last, she arose.

At once, he hastened to her side, his bow trembling in his hand. "Mother," he said, tightly, "the morning passes. If we are to reach the Ancient before the sun is high we would do well to quicken our pace."

They resumed their Northerly walk upstream, along the well-worn path that hugged the River, the trees at times drawing up to and leaning over them and at others falling back and away toward the Eastern side of the Valley. For a long while after he had spoken, she walked erect and silent, still with her hood up over her head, and did so, he noted anxiously, as was her wont - in slow, graceful steps. He felt his agitation well up within him once again and glanced, uneasily, around them at the trees to their right. At last, he could contain himself no longer.

Yet, just as he was about to burst out at her, she murmured: "I too have felt it."

He gripped his bow so hard that his right hand cried out to him in pain. He felt his heart pounding within his chest like a fist upon a hide drum.

She reached out and gripped his other arm, startling him.

"Do not banish from your thoughts the journey of your father and your brothers, Ahah-Mah," she said in a low voice from within her hood. He felt her fingers tighten upon his flesh. "Do you remember it? Do you remember where they have gone?"

He swallowed again. "Yes, Mother," he said, hollowly.

"Say it."

"In search of the River's Beginning."

"Yes," she whispered and a shiver stole through him. "At the urging of *Abba Father, Himself.*" She released her grip. "Do not forget that."

"I - " he said and stopped, sweat suddenly damp upon his forehead in the breeze coming from the North along the Valley. "We still should have brought some of the servants with us today," he muttered, not wanting to be allayed. "Even if only with their implements. Father took fifty of the men of the South with he and my brothers two dawns past and we are that much less in our ability to protect ourselves. Some should be here even now, protecting you, Mother. I can do only so much - "

"It is hardest for you, my son," she said, softly. "It has always been so. And I know that Seth is now assailed as he has never been before and that everything that we once knew and did has become perilous. But you must have Faith." She patted his arm and he felt now humiliation added to his fear.

Why could he not *believe* as did Father and Mother and his brothers - and most especially the Ancient? Why could he not banish the constant doubts from his mind? Was something not right within him? Had…... *Abba Father Himself*…...forgotten about him?

"Peace, Ahah-Mah," Mother said to him gently, as if divining his thoughts, "Peace, my son."

Yet he did not feel it. And he could not receive it from her just then - nor even, it seemed, from *Abba Father, Himself.*

Especially not this day.

They drew nigh to the fording place as the sun was gaining its zenith. There, the River shallowed and silted for a short length, allowing a crossing of its great width and then an ascent of the far, Western rise of the Valley, wherein lay the dwelling of the Ancient within its rocks.

At once, the fear and sense of danger he had had since dawn spiked through him as if he had been pierced by his own arrow!

Instinctively, Ahah-Mah reached out and seized Mother's arm, eliciting from her a sharp intake of breath. Heedless of this disrespect and driven by hot fear, he hissed at her, "Stop and stay here!" She half-raised her hand to her throat in alarm but froze where she stood, the breath caught within her hood. Bending low, he crept forward soundlessly to the side of the path and then slipped into the outlying edge of the line of trees where they drew up here and hid the last bend of the River before the fording place. Just within their silent, green hulks, he turned and cast a quick glance back at her and was grateful to see that she had not moved.

He crept amongst the bolls and through the undergrowth of the jut of the wood that thrust itself towards the curve of the River here and which forced the path to bend round it, until at last he could peek through its green foliage on the other side and see what lay beyond.

His blood ran like freezing River water through his veins when he saw. *Eneph! Here in the Valley!*

He had seen them before, of course, out on the road to the towns of the Plain, and most especially in Lod, but never this close in all his life - merely five or six long strides away! In Lod, just last Season, when Father had sent him to speak to Maskil, the cruel lord of the town, to arrange for the delivery of the year's portion of the Fruit crops, he had seen one with two of the lord's burly household slaves, towering over them as if they were but small boys and the sight had left him shaken. Ever since then, Lod, quite apart from any other town of the Plain, had become dangerous to those of Seth and if the stories that had reached his ears since he had been there were True, the *Eneph* had become even more so. He had heard it whispered amongst the servants, for Father had now forbidden he and his brothers from going to the Plain without great need, that they were coming down now out of the Grey Mountains - all of them (and who knew how many that was!) - and were even now at the Great City, Kalneh, treating with Elah-Makah himself! For some common purpose not Good, no doubt. Father did not hold with the rumour it was True but even so, the thought that former enemies of each other were now uniting against Seth, against the Valley, filled Ahah-Mah with fear.

If he had been shaken at Lod last Season at the sight of an *Eneph,* he was doubly so now. He could not breathe, for his lungs seemed to have closed in on themselves. One and then two he saw beside the River - the *River!* - the first crouched at the very edge of the broad wash of the fording place, the second standing back amongst the trees on the far side of the path, partially hidden by the low, green boughs. Both wore the great, grey over-cloaks, hiding their forms as if they were in stealth, but also marking them as dwellers of that dark and terrifying Land beyond the Plain in the East. He could not see their spears with them, those weapons which he had seen for himself were the size of small trees at least twice a man's height! It was possible that they had been left somewhere nearby with their..... Creatures.

He shuddered as he thought of those enormous beasts that were not horses.

But They cannot be here, with or without spear or creature! They cannot!

For a moment which seemed to stretch and to swallow up the swiftly-vanishing morning, nothing happened, nothing moved, and Ahah-Mah, in terror and awe, merely watched these beings who were not of the earth and yet somehow upon it, denizens more suited to the Beyond - or to the Below; these men who were not men.

Then the one nearest the River laid a hand, as huge as a man's head, within the rushing waters. "Tok oon etts dah," he spoke, staring into the waters, and his voice was a low rumble.

"Bhagra! Nosten no goort nus," said the second, more loudly, and this one's utterings were so deep and strong that they almost rumbled within Ahah-Mah himself as he crouched in the underbrush, watching them. "Tiella!"

It is the language of the Plain. They are using the tongue of the people of Elah-Makah, as sure as sure!

Yet barely. He could just recognize it for what it was but could not fully understand the words in the mouths of these creatures.

The first *Eneph* arose from the River and turned just as the second stepped forward and emerged fully from the trees and it seemed to the man watching them that they stood impossibly huge upon the earth.

The second tossed something to the first and it was this act that at last jerked Ahah-Mah out of mute astonishment and into indignation - and then to anger.

He burst out of the foliage.

"That is the Fruit of our Fathers and no others!" he shouted but he was suddenly aware of the smallness of his voice next to theirs, as if it were a child's. He felt the humiliation surge anew within him.

Both of the giants jerked their heads towards him and, at once, he was beset by two pairs of wide, smouldering, deep-set eyes beneath great, thrusting brows.

"Hah!" said the first, next the River, switching to a ghastly, guttural Valley-tongue, "is this one of them, Dawlgla? Please tell me it is."

The sound of his language, of the tongue of Seth, the Great Father, spoken by this creature, so that it sounded as if it were being spewed out of some deep hole high up in the Mountains, nettled Ahah-Mah such that he could not reply. As well, the giant's liquid, blue eyes seemed to smite him where he stood.

"Dawlgla?" repeated the first *Eneph*, eagerly, keeping his awesome, piercing gaze upon Ahah-Mah.

The second turned fully toward Ahah-Mah. This one's eyes were a gleaming, swimming green, sharp and arresting, and Ahah-Mah felt his gaze seem to pass right through him.

"Yes, Brother," rumbled Dawlgla, "this is one of the Valley-dwellers - a Sethite. I can see it in his face."

"But is it one of *his* blood," spat Bhagra, impatiently, eyes burning, "or just some worthless slave from the South?"

"We have no slaves," piped up Ahah-Mah, his bow clutched feverishly in his right hand, "like the Cities of the Plain do, only those servants who have pledged the life-bond to my Family."

He saw the *Eneph*, Bhagra, lower his gleaming eyes to his, Ahah-Mah's, right hand and then lift a massive hand toward it.

"A bow," the giant all but purred and the sound of it was like a low roll of thunder moving over the River, "In his hand, Dawlgla. Perhaps he is a great, Sethite warrior."

Dawlgla's wide lips parted into a ghastly smile. "No doubt," he growled, deep in his throat, "Perhaps even like unto the Great Father Cain himself." Ahah-Mah bristled at this. Then, Dawlgla gave a great flick of his huge head. "See there - his raiment. The white fabric of the Land of the Far River trimmed with ochre. He is, indeed, of that blood that you seek, Brother. *His* son, he is. A Prince of Seth. No less."

And then Ahah-Mah felt all of his strength and courage fail him, for Bhagra began to laugh and it was as the sound of his own death in his ears.

"A 'prince,'" spat Bhagra, "Hah! Let me kill him, Brother." His shining, blue eyes pinned Ahah-Mah to the path between the River and the trees. "Let me break his body like a dry twig and then lift it up and bear it back to the All-Father within the Mountains as an offering."

The other raised a huge hand toward him. "Not a way for a *prince* to die, Brother," said Dawlgla, in a low growl. "Not without at least bronze in his hand. Patience! Remember why we have come." Bhagra glowered at Ahah-Mah.

Dawlgla then cocked his head, fixing his own frightening, green gaze upon Ahah-Mah. "Yet there are many ways for a prince of doomed men to die," he said, in a low voice. "And this one will no doubt find his. Very soon. Right now, however," he rumbled, "I'd like to hear more about these."

And he raised up another Fruit in his huge hand so that Ahah-Mah could behold it clearly. "Tell me of this 'Fruit of our Fathers,' Sethite prince," he spat. "Does it contain Power passed on to you by your Fathers? Is it equal to that of the wild plants of our Mountains which are passed on to us by Ours? Is its Might equal to their Might? Equal to *our* might?" Again the lips spread in a hideous grin. "Can you even begin to imagine who *our* Fathers are?"

"It is an Apple," spoke Mother's firm voice and Ahah-Mah trembled when he heard it.

He spun around, heedless of all else, and beheld her stepping forward gracefully along the path from the bend of the River. "Mother!" he blurted, panicking, but she came and stood near him, flinging back her hood.

Her long, dark hair with its jagged streaks of white lay upon her shoulders but her delicately lined, copper face, Ahah-Mah saw at once, was suffused with the light of the day that was all around them so that it seemed to glow. *Or is it aglow with something else - something more?* Her dark eyes shone.

The *Eneph* became rigid. Ahah-Mah could feel it, could sense their tension even as he had been able to sense the danger earlier. For another….. *Presence*…..seemed to have come with Mother and there seemed to be a hidden striving going on within the very air around them! He felt his trembling increase.

The Fruit remained aloft in Dawlgla's enormous hand, while he, himself, flicked his great, green eyes towards Mother, a look of consternation seizing him. Bhagra emitted a low growl and actually bared his huge, grey teeth.

"And it contains much more than mere power, *Eneph*," spoke Mother and though her voice was low and even, that word on her tongue seemed to whip like a lash. "It represents Hope. Something of which you are utterly ignorant."

Bhagra flinched and snarled - a sound that shook Ahah-Mah in his very sandals - and his gleaming, blue eyes infused themselves with an angry, surging red. He reached up and flung aside his over-cloak and behold! Ahah-Mah was assailed by the mere sight of the brute's super-human body, robed in a shimmering, grey cloth from the waist down - like a *shendyt* - but with both immense chest and arms bare and rippled and corded with bulging muscle above. Ahah-Mah felt himself physically wither before this monster, felt his hands hang limply at his side, his bow slapping against his leg.

"*Our* Mothers are true Queens of Men!" screamed Bhagra and his voice seemed to assail the very trees around them. "Perfect in beauty and wisdom. *Honoured* by their sons! They are not *WITCHES!*" He was breathing hard now, like a massive bellows. He flicked his horrible red-blue eyes at Ahah-Mah. "Now you will watch as I slay your son before your eyes, Witch. With one blow of my hand!"

Then two things happened at once. Dawlgla whirled and pressed his own great hand square in the middle of Bhagra's huge, flexing chest, barking out something in their harsh, Mountain tongue. And Mother raised an arm toward Ahah-Mah.

"Cross the ford," she said to him, quietly, "Summon the Ancient. He will come. They will not stand or remain here. *Nor* will they spill blood within the Valley of Seth. Not yours. Not mine."

"Mother, you cannot stay here - !"

"I can. And I will. But I do not stand alone." The last was a fierce whisper. "Now *go!*"

Swallowing, and without a backward glance, he dashed into the River, obedient and trusting of her, as he had always been in his life, even if not fully understanding. For here was a matter of Faith, he knew, and Faith meant….. *Abba Father Himself.* He swallowed hard even as he stepped quickly across the broad, gurgling wash. *Perhaps He is here even now watching us?* The thought made him shiver. At the Western side of the Valley, he found himself Praying, fervently. '*Abba, the True Father, protect her!*'

"I am Hem-Zarah, wife of Anoh-Ah, Father of the Valley and True Son of Seth," she called out to the giants at the River-side and she spread out her long, thin, copper arms and held them up before her. "Azura is my Mother! Here I stand. What do you here within this Valley, beside this River?"

At once, both pairs of deep-set eyes facing her darted back and forth, as if taking in that Valley for the first time; taking in that River. Dawlgla's face was turned slightly toward her even as his hand remained upon his brother's chest. The Apple fell from his other hand, forgotten.

Hem-Zarah felt her heart pounding. "Do you think that I do not know who your fathers are, *Eneph?*" she cried out.

"Careful….. *Mother,*" spat Dawlgla, gazing at her over his left shoulder, and, though his eyes still burned at her, she could see that the anger had fled from the other's, for Bhagra's were now vacant and he merely stood there mute, watching them.

That's one for you, Abba Father. Your Name be praised!

"Do not be too free with that little word of yours," Dawlgla was growling at her. "Do not be too free in calling us thus or deceived into thinking that with it on your lips you have Power. You do not know what Power is, Woman. Or Fear."

She gave an involuntary shudder but kept her eyes upon his liquid, gleaming ones. *I am Yours, Abba Father. Give me strength.* "I know more than you know, Lost Son," she answered, firmly, arms still raised, heart still throbbing wildly. "I know that your Fathers were and are indeed *Eneph:* the 'Fallen Ones' of the old tales. Cast down by that True Power in all this World and in this Creation." She swallowed, dryly. "Even your 'All-Father' himself is *Eneph* - as Fallen as you are."

In a flash, Dawlgla's eyes shot through with red just as his brother's had and he smote them at her. She *felt* them. But she felt *Him* also.

Then, suddenly, they were stepping slowly backward, away from her. Away from the River.

The one named Dawlgla pushed the other named Bhagra back with a massive hand, his red-green eyes smouldering at her and his teeth bared. "It is too late, *Mother,*" he growled, "For he has already been here - the All-Father. The End is coming for you. For all of you here within this place. But first for the Ancient." His voice was like a deep hiss now and she felt herself shaking violently. "That is why we have come. To tell the Ancient to his face that the All-Father has seen his death."

Then the green boughs swung behind them and it was as if they had never been.

The words that had been flung at her like a javelin, however, still hung in the air and she continued to shake. *What was that? What did it mean?*

And she let out a long, low, trembling breath.

II

At dawn, the two men drew near once more to the cave mouth and felt the thundering spray of the gushing waters falling upon their faces.

"That is what I call a wrinkle," bellowed the first above the roar of the water. He was crouching on his haunches in the stubble at the top of the steep River-bank, and spoke around the stalk of a long, yellow reed stuck in his teeth. "A *big* one."

The second, standing beside him and squinting at the spectacle before them in the spray, gave out a long sigh and shook his head. "Still," he said just loud enough to be heard, "don't expect us to be turning around any time soon. You know Father."

"Yeah," said the first, plucking the stalk from his mouth, "I know him all right."

"And what is it that you know of him, Ajah-Phethah?" came a husky, uneven voice and the first man gave a start but then grinned, rising slowly to his feet. "Father," he said and he stepped forward, grasping a figure cloaked and hooded in a soft white fabric and lined with ochre that had just climbed the slight rise to where the two men stood upon the reed-dotted, stone River-side before the falling waters. The second man stepped forward also and did the same.

"We were merely enjoying the dawn's light in the mists of the waters, Father, and speaking of how we knew you would like to behold it in the day-time," spoke the second man, somewhat placatingly, resting his hand upon the figure's arm.

The figure straightened himself to his full height and, breathing heavily, reached up and flung back his hood revealing a wide, copper-coloured, grey-bearded face with slight lines around twinkling, light-brown eyes. "That," he said, "I very much doubt, Asheh-Mah."

Ajah-Phethah gave out a laugh at this and slapped his brother, playfully, on the arm. "Actually, Asheh-Mah here was just telling me about how this was all a part of your Master Plan, Father. To bring us and half the servants and pack animals to a remote place and set up another, new Household of Seth - one far from Cain."

"Hmmm," said the old man and worried lines suddenly creased his forehead but the twinkle did not leave his eyes. "If only that were possible, My Sons, but I fear that such a feat would be all but impossible these days - however Heroic they might be. Seth could not accomplish this. Even the *Eneph* could not do so, for all the world is no longer big enough and the Sons of that Father are never far anymore."

Asheh-Mah clicked his teeth, deprecatingly. "If I had Truly said anything like that, Father, it would have been only to curse that man and all his sons."

"Hush!" said Father, turning on Asheh-Mah, "Such pronouncements are best left to the One who alone can stand by them. Hmmm?" And he shot out his bristling, grey brows at both of them. "And that man is still Father to many in this world. Ours is to live in Peace and Regard always as far as it depends upon us - even with the Sons of Cain if that be still possible. Is that understood by my stubborn children?"

"It is, Father," said Ajah-Phethah, quickly, and Asheh-Mah nodded, lowering his eyes.

"Now then," said Father, sucking in a deep breath and the spray of the waters was damp upon his face, "let us take a closer look at what we have found before us by the light of day, shall we?"

He began to step in the direction of the gushing waters along the top of the River-side and his two sons shot out their arms to help support him upon its uneven, reedy, rocky ground.

"Where on earth is your stick, Father?" scolded Asheh-Mah.

The old man waved his hand, dismissively. "Aaaah!" he grumbled.

"It is right here!" called out a deep voice from behind and below them and all three turned to watch another man climb the rise from the clutch of hide tents that crouched amongst the patches of small trees in the Valley's dwindling Eastern side. "Master Anoh-Ah left it behind as usual."

Father regarded the man, eyes shining. "Traitor," he grunted. "A-Phthah the Wet-Nurse I should call you."

The other man gained the River-side height and stood amongst them. He was dark-skinned and clean-shaven and his black hair was cut short all around his head. He held out in his long, thin arms a staff of acacia wood with a flat grip.

Reluctantly, Anoh-Ah took it from him. "Very well, very well!" he said, grumpily. "Now help me down to that ledge there if you must." He pointed the tip of his stick toward a narrow shelf of rock that jutted out almost right over the moving, churning water itself, not twenty strides downstream from the falling cascade of the River gushing out of the cave in the rock.

"I will take you, Father," bellowed Asheh-Mah, holding out his hand, but the old man shook his head. "No, I want A-Phthah with me there." He looked at the darker man, brows raised expectantly.

"As you say, Master," said A-Phthah, somewhat puzzled, and he grasped Anoh-Ah's arm and together the two of them made their way, carefully, down to the rock ledge. The others watched them anxiously, Ajah-Phethah shaking his head, a wry smile on his face, but Asheh-Mah tense and rigid.

"Tell me what you see, Old Friend," whispered the older man in his ear and A-Phthah at once emerged fully from the fog that had clung to him since he had arisen that dawn. Strange dreams and images had come to him overnight, with the sound of the waters ever in the background, and they had left him muddle-headed. He had almost missed the fact that the Master had left behind his staff.

But now he calls me 'Friend' and that can mean only one thing.

It had started mere months ago when Master Anoh-Ah had begun calling him 'Friend.' It had grated on him at first, he had had to admit. It was unseemly. He was Head of the Household servants, in both Home and Field, but he was not 'Friend' to the First Family of Seth. This implied privileges and honours that were not his, the like of which made him uncomfortable. Yet, always in secret, always whenever the ears of the rest of the Family were not around, did the Master call him thus - as if the Master himself wanted to bestow these favours upon him in his own heart.

A-Phthah had also quickly come to learn that 'Friend' meant that a secret was coming. A secret from *Abba Father* to the Master, which the Master, in turn, wanted to share with him to see how he would receive it. It seemed that *Abba Father* was speaking more and more often to the Master these days but it was not known why. Oh, for some great, great purpose - of that there could be no doubt - but it was as yet…..unknowable. And the greatest secret thus far had been that which had led them to this very place.

So it was now. He knew it. He felt it.

The Master had received another Message.

So what is it that I see?

Closing his eyes, he forced himself to clear his mind and his heart. First, he took in a deep breath of the moist air over the River. *I smell the cave, all right. Deep, deep within rock that reaches far, far into the earth.* He shivered but not from the cold. *The River flows here from far, far away. And its source is hidden.*

He snapped open his eyes. He was aware of the Master watching him closely. Slowly, he moved his eyes to regard the waterfall in all its might and then the cave, itself, a wide, dark mouth splitting the rock from which the River gushed. Raising his eyes, he took in the high, sheer cliff looming above it, above them all, beyond which nothing was visible, only the brilliant blue of the sky above. Panning his gaze to the left, to the West, he saw the arms of the cliff lowering to the far side of the River, where tumbles and tangles of reeds and weeds dwelt, at times falling to the very edge of the swiftly-flowing, foaming water itself.

Hidden.

"It is a barrier," he murmured in the other man's ear after a long while, "a barrier not just for the eyes but for the body. To block any from entering the Valley from without. To protect all those within from great numbers without."

"Hmmm," pondered the other man, listening. Then he nodded. "Yes," he murmured in reply, "The Succour of Seth by the Hand of *Abba Father*. But now, Old Friend, Seth must leave the Valley." The trembling seized A-Phthah again and he wrapped his long arms around himself within his cloak. "This he has been called to do - *we* have been called to do. After many, many years uncounted and many, many Fathers, Seth must rise up out of the Valley. He must leave his home behind."

A-Phthah swallowed hard. "Where will he go, I wonder?" he murmured and he hugged himself tighter. The thought terrified him.

"All of this," the Master was saying, sweeping his arm toward the crashing waters and the high cliff wall above them, "causes us to rely only upon Him for the way. The South you know, for you are from it, Dear

Friend. Seth is not called that way for he did not *come* from that way. The East is lost, the West is barred by cliffs. And now the North is blocked too. You, yourself, have said it: where then will he go?"

A-Phthah heard a quaver of excitement in his Master's voice and he turned to regard him. "If there is a way beyond *this*, Master," he said, gesturing also, and leaning conspiratorially closer to the other, "then it is hidden from your servant."

A wide smile split Anoh-Ah's face then and he grinned like a boy. "Yes!" he exclaimed, "Exactly!" And he even rubbed his thin hands together with glee. "Hidden even in plain sight! Now.....here's what I want you to do. I want you to go back at once into the camp and bring to me two strong, young lads. And make sure that they are short." He held up his hand, palm flat, at the level of his chest.

A-Phthah gave a start. "I'm sorry, Master, but did you say.....*short?*"

It was all Anoh-Ah could do to keep from bursting. A-Phthah cloud see spasms begin to shake the older man and in the end all the Master could do was to give a quick, jerky nod.

With a sigh, A-Phthah shrugged and turned to go back the way he had come. Sometimes the old man's games just seemed to elude him. "As you say, Master."

Within a short while, the two brothers stood with A-Phthah atop the River-side gazing pensively down at the old man and the two youths standing on the rock shelf below them. Ajah-Phethah was again crouched on his haunches with a reed stuck in his mouth, Asheh-Mah standing beside him. The two lads below were indeed short: both scarcely came up to Anoh-Ah's stooped shoulders. They could see him talking animatedly with them but the waters' roar was all that could be heard.

"What's all this about, then?" mused Ajah-Phethah. He swivelled his eyes up to his brother's. "Still a part of the Plan?"

Asheh-Mah gave a snort. "If there *is* any Master Plan around here, Brother, it is tucked so far away in that mysterious, old head down there that not even *Abba Father* could wiggle it out."

"He is the One who told it," burst out A-Phthah then, watching the figures on the rock shelf below, the spray sheening his face, "*Abba Father* has told the Master the way beyond. I know He has. The way out of the Valley."

There was only the sound of the cascade for a long time and the other two turned to stare at him.

"Off you go then!" bellowed Anoh-Ah and the two youths stared at one another for an instant, a look of terror etched on their faces. Then they swallowed and turned as one toward the immense spout of thundering water and watched it for a long moment as if frozen to the rock where they stood. At last, steeling themselves as if for battle, they began to step along the grey, rocky shelf toward it.

The three atop the River-side watched silently as the two youths began moving along the rock shelf. They watched them step across the wet stone farther and farther until suddenly they disappeared.

Into the very falling water itself!

Ajah-Phethah shot to his feet, the reed falling from his mouth. "What the - ?"

Asheh-Mah's mouth hung open. "By *Abba Father Himself!*"

But A-Phthah laughed and struck his leg. "I knew it! I knew something was going to happen! Hidden in plain sight!"

Down below them, Father was laughing into the spray and they could see even from where they stood that his light, brown eyes were dancing in the sunlight that was now just peeking over the Eastern edge of the Valley.

After what seemed an age, or of at least a Seasons-Turn, during which it seemed to those standing atop the River-side that the sun actually climbed noticeably behind them, the two youths appeared on the far side of the River! They waved excitedly across the spray and Anoh-Ah waved back. Their faces were slick with spray. That could be seen from clear across the River, yet it did not look as if their tunics or breeches were wet.

"Excellent, excellent!" they could hear Anoh-Ah shouting. "A-Phthah! Get down here! We have work to do!"

The old servant jumped and began stepping down to the rock shelf.

Behind him, the brothers turned to face each other. "The Master Plan," said Ajah-Phethah, in wonder.

The Rise was narrow. Its narrowness and hiddenness astonished Ajah-Phethah. As he walked back down to where Father was climbing, with its tall, dry grasses brushing against his lower legs, he could not help gazing back and forth between both of its high, sheer walls of rock that loomed over them, to both East and West. They could not be more than twenty strides apart, he judged. He shook his head in wonder. They had all entered another valley, this one leading steadily up, of grass and stone.

The rock shelf that had lined both sides of the River at the waterfall had been in parts wide enough for even the pack animals to walk on it with ease! It had been utterly hidden from the eyes from the higher level of the River-side but from the rock shelf it had been clearly visible if you knew how to look for it. Ajah-Phethah had seen with his own eyes how only the finger of *Abba Father Himself* could have wrought such a thing!

All of them, the Family - or at least that part that had come here, the fifty servants, and the dozen pack animals had all passed along the shelf, deep into the rock behind the falling waters into a labyrinth of damp passages, and then had finally emerged along the Western side of the River, the spray touching their faces but not wetting their cloaks or tunics! Then, after only a few dozen paces along the Western side of the River, through hanging boughs and weeds, they had found the entrance to this rise, this new 'Valley of Stone.' The sound of the falling water had become muted by then and before they knew it, beginning the climb between the high, rocky walls, they seemed to be passing up toward a whole, new, unknown world.

Ajah-Phethah, panting slightly, at last reached Father, who was walking with A-Phthah, the rest of the men, with Asheh-Mah, and the animals arrayed behind and below them. Father was thrusting the heel of his staff into the tall grasses with each step as they ascended. Fortunately, Ajah-Phethah reflected, the ascent between the cliffs was gradual enough to allow for a manageable climb for both man and laden beast.

"I've got twelve men up ahead, some fifty paces above us," he said to Father, "With full quivers and with bronze at their sides as well. Artuah will sound his horn if there is the slightest incident. But there's no end to this trough between these stone walls for as far as I could see above us, Father." He shook his head. "Where on earth are we going?"

Anoh-Ah swallowed and looked past him up the Rise. He stopped and A-Phthah paused beside him. At once, all who were behind did so as well, the servants pulling back on the animals' leads, making them almost rear back. "I do not know, My Son," Anoh-Ah whispered, "That, He has not shown to me, nor has He given me any Sign yet of the way ahead. The next step I do not know. I know only that we must walk in Faith. We must not

Fear, *never* Fear, for that is the province of Cain and his baleful son who sits in fell splendour at Kalneh and whose arm is even now stretching farther and farther out over this entire world. *NO!"* Anoh-Ah gave a vigorous shake of his white head and his light, brown eyes glinted. Both of his sons, for Asheh-Mah had now come forward and joined them, swallowed hard as they listened to him. "We must trust *Him*. And Him alone."

"Even so," said A-Phthah with passion and then they were all saying it, up and down the line - all of the servants, both older and younger.

Ajah-Phethah felt his heart beat faster. *Truth,* he thought.

They continued their climb, pausing whenever they needed to, until the sun was high overhead and shone straight down at them between the shoulders of rock. The animals began to wicker and Asheh-Mah, who had resumed his spot at the rear, now came forward and rejoined them again, for Ajah-Phethah had remained with Father and A-Phthah. No sound of Artuah's horn had yet been heard. "Let us rest for a while," said Father then. He turned to Ajah-Phethah. "Recall the men," he told him. "We will all eat a meal together."

When they were all gathered, seated upon the tall, dry grass in that valley of stone between the high cliffs, the brothers with A-Phthah facing up the Rise toward the North and all the servants, including the scouts who had gone ahead, and the animals arrayed behind them, Anoh-Ah took a loaf of hard, spelt bread that his wife Hem-Zarah had baked with her own hands for them two days before and held it up before them all, standing in front of them.

"This bread was made by the Mistress for me and my sons using the last remnants of ingredients gotten from the Plain in exchange for our Fruit," he said to them. "There will be no more bread for Seth obtained in this fashion - for Lod, the Towns and Cities, all the Plain, is now closed to him." He looked around at them. "Even all the world." He lifted the bread higher. "But we will eat it now. Together. *All* of us. For I believe that there is a promise of another bread to come. Not from the Plain. Not from the world. But from - " He broke off, unable to continue, and he lowered the bread and tore off a small piece of it. After this he went and, breaking off another, handed it to Asheh-Mah, who accepted it silently. Another went to Ajah-Phethah and then the rest of the loaf went to A-Phthah who at first would not take it but when the Master had entreated him with moist eyes, he took it and began tearing off pieces for all of the servants.

They ate together, quietly, and then there came a great sigh of wind through the valley from the North. It had a bite of cold that they had never before felt back in the Valley of Seth and all of them turned to gaze up the long, narrow way between the walls of rock. Overhead, torn and tattered clouds could be seen passing over the gap between the high, stone shoulders above them.

Anoh-Ah drew his cloak tighter about himself and then raised his right hand over them all. *"Abba Father!"* he cried, "Lead us. Guide us. Go out before us, walk with us, and come behind us. We go toward the Promise of a new world. Help us to walk in Faith."

"Even so!" gasped Asheh-Mah.

Anoh-Ah grasped his staff. "Now we must go," he said, "and we must not stop until we find what He has set before us."

In the late afternoon, now climbing with great weariness, something around them began to change. The Eastern, right wall of rock began to lower, at first almost imperceptibly, but then more and more noticeably until finally it fell away completely, revealing to them a vista so vast it overwhelmed them!

They paused, stunned, and all were silent, staring wide-eyed. Master Anoh-Ah staggered to the very edge of the immensity, his staff thrusting deep into the dry grasses and dust and stone of the ground. Asheh-Mah and Ajah-Phethah came and steadied him, standing beside him.

Together they looked out over the vastness in the East.

Below them, far, far below at the foot of the enormous, sheer cliff atop which they stood, stretched all the world.

"It is the whole Plain," murmured Asheh-Mah, "and far away, *there,* at the edge of the world, I can see the Grey Mountains. Look!" He shivered within his cloak.

"And look there!" added Ajah-Phethah, thrusting a finger toward the NorthEast. "I see a river stretching down out of the North. Could it be….. the River? Ours?"

Anoh-Ah took in a deep breath. "It is the Land of our enemies and of all those who have set themselves up against *Him,* My Sons." He said this in a low voice and the high, cool wind carried his words away over the lands below them. "It is grown now very large," he went on, "yet how He longs to reach out and grasp it, and hold it to Himself even still. But He cannot. It has forsaken Him - even as has all this world. The world that *He* made."

They could see the grey shape of a Town situated not far from the foot of their high cliff and much farther away, the much larger, sprawling shape of the Great City, itself, seeming to lie half in light and half in darkness across the very edge of the SouthEastern horizon. When Father had uttered these words, the sons found their eyes drawn inexorably toward this massive shape, their hearts pounding in their temples.

In the middle of the City, just at the edge of the world, stood a vast, stone Ziggurat, in both darkness and light, tall and brazen, like a great, multi-staired, multi-storied, stone plinth thrust up defiantly toward the Beyond.

Anoh Ah trembled.

"Come," he said, firmly, "we must go now. We cannot pause any longer."

They resumed their slow climb, the Plain beside and far below them. All were bent now and the animals seemed to lower their heads and plod forward under the hands of those who led them as if steeling themselves for a last effort.

And then, only minutes later, the second wonderful event happened.

They reached level ground. And as they seemed to attain the apex of their ascent, it was now the Western stone wall that fell swiftly into the very ground and they found themselves at the very Eastern end of another wide valley of tall, yellow grass on the very roof of the world! This one stretched out in the direction of the now lowering sun. Two spines of mountains with sloping, lowering foothills lined this new valley to both North and South.

Yet this was not the whole of the wonder - for once more they heard the muted sound of rushing water!

At once, Asheh-Mah and Ajah-Phethah rushed to Father's side and A-Phthah stood nearby. All were panting from the climb and, although the sound of water was unmistakable, they could as yet see nothing ahead or beside them that would give them a clue as to its source.

"What does it mean?" asked Ajah-Phethah, almost breathlessly.

Father turned to look at him, light brown eyes twinkling once more. "It means that we must exercise Patience, My Son. This, you, in particular, must still learn." He raised a finger, scoldingly, at him.

"Wait," interjected Asheh-Mah. "Something is strange."

Father and Ajah-Phethah broke off their talk and looked out all around them. They were still breathing labouredly, no longer from the climb, but from the very thinness of the cooler, higher air itself.

Asheh-Mah pointed out over the new, high, yellow valley. "The grasses are below us yet. Do you see? Not far, far below but definitely lower. How do we get down there from here? Is that where the sound of the water is coming from? I hope there is not another cliff."

Ajah-Phethah gave out a laugh. "Father? That would be your area of expertise, no?"

They went on, breathing hard.

"By *Abba Father!*" cried Asheh-Mah, then. "Look! Another river!"

And so it was. They saw a river flowing toward them, following the line of the Southern foothills that ran away to the West before them. It lined the new valley's Southern edge, in the very shadow of those foothills, and had hidden itself from them until this moment. But not only toward them did it flow - but right beneath them!

For Behold! They stood now upon the roof of a stone wall into which this new river flowed through a great rent far below their feet.

And it was the old river - the River of Seth!

There could be no doubt.

"Oh, my," said Anoh-Ah, stepping carefully with his staff to the edge of the wall upon which they stood and looking down at the rushing water beneath them. The two brothers could see tears shining in his eyes from the light of the sun lowering before them from the far end of the new valley. "Now we know whence the River flows into the Valley," he said in awe. Slowly, he looked up and saw its winding, silver thread, rushing from the West. "But from where does it Begin, this, we do not yet know. But we shall." He looked around at his sons. "This is the next step. We must find the way down and then follow the sun to the start of the River."

"And what we shall find then?" whispered A-Phthah, behind them. *"Abba Father Himself?"*

III

When had the journey begun? It had been so long ago now, he could not remember. In Truth, there were two journeys. (He nodded his weary head at the thought.) His own. *Yes. Absolutely.* That one was long enough. But there was also the journey of Seth, the Great Father, himself, and that was longer still. And it was likely to extend beyond his.

And yet!

Abba Father, teach me. What are you speaking of when you bring the two journeys to my thoughts?

He coughed deep down in his chest and opened his bleary eyes. He winced. The sun's brightness and position told of mid-morning yet he did not remember waking. Frowning, he crouched in the maw of his dwelling, looking out upon the Valley laid out before his door. And below, the River ran past.

He felt his frown disappear as he looked down at it. Oh, he could remember gazing at the River for hours at a time when he was a small boy and his family would come down to it; could remember the sun striking its rippling crests and dazzling his young, eager eyes! Father would be irate at those times and would call him a lazy-bones. Most often because he held up their return to the Plain and there was nothing like the River upon that part of the Plain where they dwelt. He smiled with the long-ago thought.

But then the frown returned and settled deeply in the lines of his face again. Was that a True memory or did he only imagine a small boy who loved to spend his days at the River-side a thousand Season-Turns ago?

He shook his head. Sometimes it ached.

The Beginning is the End.

He jumped. *What in the Name - ? Where did that come from?*

But, at once, he was whispering, raggedly, "…..and the End is the Beginning."

His heart beat faster so that it ached like his head.

It was what *Abba Father* had been teaching him! Trembling, he sharpened his gaze and cocked his ears, trying to *see* and to *hear* in case there should be more that would come.

But the Valley was the same as it had always been. The River flowed as it always had.

He sighed and felt now all of the aches of his tired body. *Ah, Abba Father, I will not fret. You are Good. It will all come in its time.*

"Even so," he croaked and his mouth felt dry. *I must fetch more water from the River.*

Slowly, he rose but his body creaked and teetered. *"Abba Father!"* he moaned in pain, flailing his arm out to catch himself before he fell flat on his face upon the stone floor. *I can't do this anymore, crouching here like this. My grandson and his sons can do it but not me any longer. Or have I been at it too long this day and just can't remember?*

Grasping the rock of the side of his dwelling and grunting, he hauled himself half to his feet - which was all that he could manage these days - and spotted the clay ewer with its clay vessel in the dark corner of the cave entrance, where the sun's mid-morning rays no longer quite reached. He shuffled over to them and went to lift the ewer. With a grunt of surprise he felt at once by its coolness and its heaviness that it was already quite full.

"Why, someone must have filled it," he rasped, bewildered.

No…..wait. He had done so. He had filled it while it had been still dark because it had been needed. Was that another day or this one? He shook his head. It was all a blur lately. So much activity! The needs of his guest…..

His guest!

"Oh, *Abba Father,* forgive me!" he groaned, "I have been a foolish old man, wallowing in my meanderings, and have neglected the poor child!"

Panting, and with shaking hands, he hefted the ewer and took up the vessel. Staggering through the narrow passage with them, he passed into the wider living area of the cave. Here, the dry grass mats stirred beneath his bare feet and, upon the far wall, shone a round shaft of sunlight that came through the rent in the rock ceiling. Beneath it, against the far wall, lay a low bed consisting mostly of pelts of fur, both old and new, from the many small creatures of the Valley that, from days no longer counted, he had hunted with his javelin.

Some of the blankets and heavy cloaks came also from his grandson's Household but his own beloved over-cloak itself was wrapped snugly around a slight figure that lay unmoving upon the crude bed.

Slowly, carefully, grunting with the effort, he set the ewer and the vessel down next to the pallet and leant over it. She was still sleeping, one arm resting upon his cloak. By the shaft of sunlight, he could see that the sallowness that had clung to the ebon skin of her body and of her face these last two days had at last left it. Her breath was still ragged, though, coming fitfully from her nostrils, but it was stronger than it had been only the night before. *Is it only two days since I found her out there, her blood upon the rocks…..?*

He swallowed hard and gritted his teeth against the horribleness of it. The image of the girl's broken body, lying upon the large rocks just upstream from the Wash, in a pool of blood.

As if she had been gored. As if she had been *attacked!*

In the Valley of Seth itself.

He had staggered on his feet as if struck a blow in the face when he had come across her, unable to process what he was seeing. He swallowed, nervously, again.

Yes, in the Valley. It could not be denied. And what was more, there had been nothing of its like here within the Home of Seth since he had first come to dwell in it these many, many years. Since the Master of its present Household had wrenched his leg as a young lad nothing had even approached it, and *that* had been but a paltry thing next to this!

Frowning, he looked down upon his mysterious, young guest for a while, listening to her rough breathing. *Is the Valley losing its protection? Is this one not of its Master's Household and therefore beneath the hem of the garment of the Great Father?* Reaching out a trembling hand, he placed it gently upon her brow. He let out a sigh of relief as he discovered that her fever had also passed with the night. Her skin was still damp but it no longer burned to the touch. "*Abba Father,* be praised," he whispered. "You, you alone have healed her thus far."

She stirred and gave out a low moan, startling him. He turned, at once, to the ewer and dipped the vessel within it, drawing out some of the cool water.

Her arm upon the cloak was jerking up towards her face.

"Gentle," he said, quickly, "It is the water vessel, Child. Take some. Carefully now." He touched the vessel to her cheek and waited as her hand fumbled toward it and caught hold of it. With his other hand, he slightly elevated her head and she turned it and helped guide the water to her cracked, parched lips.

A low moan came from her again and she licked her lips with a swollen tongue. She coughed slightly.

"More?" he asked and when she nodded weakly, he let her drink two more quick swallows. "That's good for now," he said, gently, and she lay back again. He set the vessel down next to the ewer.

Her dark eyes fluttered open in the dimness and looked around at him. He could see them in the dull light of the cave.

Suddenly, he gasped, "Hed-Nah! You've come back! Where have you been all this time?" Impulsively, he reached out again and this time touched her long, dark, matted hair.

But just as quickly he withdrew his hand as if it had touched a hot flame.

The eyes were not Hed-Nah's. They were not his wife's.

How could I have been so foolish? She died so long ago, didn't she? So long. And now she walks with Him. How could she be here, still within this dim place bereft of the Glory that is now hers? "I - I am sorry, My Child," he stammered. "I mistook you - "

But the dark eyes had now opened wide with awe. "You are Akad-Amon," the girl rasped. "I dreamt about you."

A wide smile burst out on his face and the burden of all of the horribleness of her affliction suddenly lifted from him. "Ah, to you indeed, I am Akad-Amon, My Dear," he chuckled. "The 'Ancient,' in Truth. For none now live in this world who have seen the Seasons that I have seen." He laughed freely, albeit wheezily, then, as he had not done in a long while and did so until his ribs ached along with the rest of him. "No doubt your Master has called me thus to you, hmm? And to all of the South as well. He is, though almost six hundred Season-Turns himself, but a whelp next to me." *Abba, You are Good to let an old man have such fun at his own expense.*

But the mention of Anoh-Ah had made the girl anxious. "My Master," she croaked, trying to rise, "and my Mistress - they will punish me."

He shot out a hand to restrain her. "Hush, now. Be still." His admonishment was gentle but firm. "I will have none of that here. You are my guest and under my charge now." He raised his bristled brows at her and he felt her settle down again beneath the over-cloak. "Now," he said, stridently, "What is your name, Child? For I still have not heard it, even after two days, because of your grievous hurt. You have been scarcely awake in all that time."

She swallowed and he saw her wince slightly. Licking her lips again, she whispered, "I am called Neltamuk." She lowered her eyes from his. "I am Daughter to Na-Eltuk and Ar-Ebab. I belong to the Household of Anoh-Ah, Son of Seth."

He looked at her kindly. "You are indeed of the Household of Anoh-Ah, who honours his servants, for he does not treat them as do the Lords of the Plain. Hmm? He will not punish where punishment is unwarranted. Yes?"

Abashed, she darted her eyes back to his and gaped up at him for a moment before nodding silently. "Yes, Sir," she whispered. "He is Good. I have seen it. But I have been Bad. I went out to the River in search of our pup and went too far. And the sun sank into the earth. And I slipped by night and fell down to the rocks. I - I - "

And she winced sharply this time, gritting her teeth and stifling a moan. He saw her almost double up beneath the cloak.

"Here now!" he said, urgently. "Lie still!" He reached out again and held her head down upon the crude bundle of hides beneath it. "Breathe," he told her. "Just breathe."

She lay still again and he heard her take in a deep breath and then let it out slowly and raggedly.

"Yes," he said, more gently, "even so."

A minute longer, she breathed and he sat beside her. Then he said to her, "Child - Neltamuk, Daughter of Na-Eltuk and Ar-Abab, of the Household of Anoh-Ah, Son of Seth - I must look at your wound."

It was as if a convulsion seized her for her entire body jerked taut and her hand slammed down upon the over-cloak, her dark fingers clutching it so tightly that they were as white. A long wail came from her lips. *"ABBA! Save me!"* she screamed, hoarsely.

And he knew that she was there in that moment again. Alone in the dark and suffering pain that he could not imagine.

And something was with her.

He gave a jerk and frowned again, his whole body quivering.

Something insidious was with her there. In the Valley of Seth, by night.

The quivering became a shudder and he desperately grabbed a hold of her clenched hand upon the cloak and brought his forehead down to it.

He Prayed with all his might.

The sun was gaining its zenith and beat down hard upon the Valley. He could feel the sweat trickling down his neck as he crouched within the maw of his dwelling once more.

His heart still raced inside his chest.

"Abba Father, what you said to me there next the bed just now frightens me," he spoke aloud, brokenly, to the Valley. "Why did you show it to me?"

HE was departing the Valley.

This he was shown, this he saw. *Abba Father's* voice had spoken within his mind and within his heart as he had Prayed for the girl. Seth was to follow his God, the One True God, out of the Valley. The Enemy, sensing this, *feeling* this, was moving - had *been* moving. Oh, yes. The final confrontation between the Brothers, of Cain and of Seth, long-estranged, long-sundered from time immemorial, was coming at last - and coming swiftly. The girl was proof of this. Brought to his very door.

And all the world would tremble in the final reckoning!

For the two could no longer live together upon the same Earth. Cain. And Seth. Everything and everyone would be caught up in their inextricable Fates. The Valley as well as the Plain. All of it would end.

And then begin again.

He swallowed, dryly, and looked, dazedly, upon the River. Absently, he shook his head. He still did not understand the fullness of it. Only that it was Truth - Truth from *Abba Father Himself.* And he had been told another Truth also. *Oh, yes.* He had been told that he himself would not live to see this new 'Beginning.' This - the nearing end of his own journey - he had long felt in his guts and in his heart for many a Season-Turn now, but this word from *Abba Father* confirmed it. It almost gave him joy. Yes. He nodded to himself. Joy even in spite of not seeing the new Beginning.

Yet his guest!

A thrill went through him and he jerked out of his reverie and wincing, got up and returned at once within the cave to her side. Her healing now was his paramount duty.

His last one.

He was surprised to find her awake, for when the Darkness had touched her (oh, there was no doubt now what had happened when he had tried to see her wound and she had cried out to Him with all her might) and had tried to scare her again she had seemed so utterly spent afterward that she had collapsed unconscious once more upon the pallet. With a sudden spike of terror through his chest, he had thought her quite dead! But no. She had slept only but he had been so shaken that he had had to leave her and Pray further outside.

Now, she whispered roughly to him as he approached, "It is okay, Akad-Amon. I can bear now for it to be seen. I feel…..better."

"You are brave, Child," he told her, "Braver than you know. And you will bear far more than this in the great days to come."

He could see her frowning slightly at him in the dimness at this. "What do you mean?" she whispered.

He managed a trembling smile and knelt down once more beside her.

"I mean," he answered, fervently, "only that you need not be troubled ever again if you put your Faith and Trust in Him, the God of Seth, from this day forward. Always. Do you promise to do this? Tell me you will!"

She swallowed and nodded up at him. "I will," she whispered.

At once, he sighed and some of the tension that had crept into his body left it again. Still, he trembled slightly. *Will the Enemy plot to attack her again?* He tightened his jaw against the thought. "Now then……," he said firmly and he reached out and lifted the over-cloak, gently drawing it down almost to her hips. Her upper body was wrapped in the many blankets but her midriff was bare and wrapped only in drying strips of cloth. He saw at once that the newest ones that he had applied before dawn were grey and not stained dark with crimson blood as the old ones had been only the night before.

"Praise *Abba Father,*" he whispered.

She was trembling noticeably and breathing shallowly, staring up at the ceiling.

"Do not fear, Child," he said, carefully lifting the strips.

She groaned softly as the cloth pulled from her skin and he grimaced at his own clumsiness. With one hand he dipped the vessel in the ewer and very slowly cleansed the wound with cool water.

She gasped and shuddered, clutching at the over-cloak.

"Good, good," he said, "Very good." He wiped the wound gently. It was a dull, closed cut-mark now, still raw, but no longer the scary gash that it had been. Yet, in the dimness, something did not look quite right about it. Frowning, he bent down and looked more closely at it.

He let out a low, humming breath.

"What is it, Sir?" she said in a low voice, still looking up at the rock of the ceiling above. He could hear the tension in it. "Is it not healed?"

"Although the wound itself is closed, My Dear," he said quietly, "there is an area of dull grey all around it which concerns me. It is altogether different from the colour of your healthy skin. I fear there has been….. hurt inside your body. That we cannot see." Carefully, he felt with his fingertips around the wound, gently prodding her abdomen.

She winced and gave out another groan, clutching the over-cloak more tightly than before. Her breath caught in her throat for a heartbeat and then came raggedly after.

He straightened.

"You have been touched by the Enemy," he said, turning to her and at last she moved her gaze from the ceiling and met his. He saw the fear enter into her widening, dark eyes and he felt suddenly a burgeoning rage sweep over him. His withered hands curled into tight, painful fists at his side, but he hid them from her. "When you fell, Neltamuk, Daughter of Na-Eltuk and Ar-Abab," he said through clenching teeth, "that branch….. impaled you right there. *Right -* " He choked with fury and had to look away for a moment before meeting her eyes again. "He tried to steal away the Fruit of your Mothers, Child," he whispered, fiercely. "The gift that they have given to you. He tried to make you barren."

She stared at him. "M-My Mistress tells us that we are all daughters of Azura," she murmured, after a while. "My mother and me and all the servant-girls - that all women of Seth are the Great Mother's heirs."

He drew in a deep breath and gave his anger deliberately to *Abba Father. Take it, My God. Take it unto Yourself for it is You who fight for us against the Enemy. I cannot do it. I must help her.* "The daughter of the Great Mother you are," he told her, firmly. "For do not her heirs inhabit all of the South and the Valley?" He lifted a gnarled finger and pointed it warningly at her. "Do not forget that. And yet you must not forget either that even the Great Mother herself had a mother! The mother of all of the living that one was and indeed even the mother of Cain."

The girl gasped.

"In the end we are all *HIS* children. Yes?"

She nodded, her mouth agape.

Then he was looking away again, lost in thought. "I remember, indeed, her place - the place of our Great Mother, Azura," he murmured, absently.

Her jaw dropped. "You have seen the Great Mother!" she croaked.

He snapped his eyes back to her with a start. "Oh! No - no, Child. I saw only the place where she was laid - her tomb beneath the stones. Far away in the North of the Plain it was. Perhaps it is even there still. A great Cairn. When I was but a small child I laid eyes on it."

Slowly, she reached down and raised the over-cloak up to her chin again. The wound was left as it was but he sat back on the bottoms of his feet and let her do what she would.

"Tell me," she said. "It - it takes away the pain."

He smiled at her again and tears sprang into his eyes. Quickly, he wiped them away. "I would be honoured to tell you," he said, "for I see now that what the Great Mother began, you will continue. For will you not also be the mother of many? Will not nations come from you?"

Her mouth fell open again at this but she remained silent, watching him, expectantly.

He took a breath. "Just as I am now," he said, quietly, "so was the Great Mother before I was born. Amongst other things, she too was 'great' with age, seeing almost a thousand Season-Turns before even I was born." He chuckled. "None else in all the world in her time had seen such Years and as long as she lived, our enemies on the Plain held her in high fear and let those villages of Seth well alone. For she was also 'great' in Faith and Wisdom. She knew *HIM*. Yes?"

He saw his guest nod silently, gaze rapt.

"Now my own father told me of the time when Seth dwelt in many villages in the North of the Plain. But when the Great Mother at last passed into *Abba Father's* Glory and they laid her in that tomb far away, the Sons of Cain threw off their fear and made war upon the Sons of Seth and pushed them into the South until at last Seth dwelt in one village only." He held up a single, withered finger into the air. "In those days also the *Eneph* arose and made themselves known and went away into the dark shadows of their far Mountains in the East. Those that are called 'Grey.' That is when I came to the Valley. Many of Seth had already gone away into the South long before. I myself had already my own family then." He paused, looking down at her, the smile trembling upon his lips. "Your Master was then but a small boy - " He broke off.

"AKAD-AMON! AKAD-AMON! Come quickly! There is danger within the Valley! Danger!"

"Ah!" said the old man to the girl upon the pallet. "Your Master's son is here!" His gaze held her intently. "And I perceive that he will find more here than he was expecting to find for I see now the Hand of *Abba Father* in all of this. Come, Child, we must heal your body first. It is what *HE* tells me now."

Drawing close to the pallet, he reached out and clasped her hand and once more Prayed.

IV

She gazed into the polished bronze and delicately applied the *akhulah* to her eyes. Afterward, she set down the small, black stick and sat back appraising herself. The deep blue of her irises glinted sharply in the light of the oil lamp upon her table and within her smooth, copper-skinned face.

Ah, now they pierce, don't they? Had-Ahah, your lord and husband will look into your eyes and feel helpless before you!

She smiled.

Her adversary had not her eyes. No. They were her weapons, her Power, alone. That *other* woman came from a far, uncouth country in the distant North. Upjumped. Dirty. Oh, she had Power of a different kind. Had-Ahah gritted her teeth as she beheld herself in the flawless, bronze mirror. She could not deny this, for it struck at the very heart of what it was to be a Woman. Her lord and husband was too much of a Man for his own good. He could not see the vileness of her adversary's deceit and was enslaved by that shameless person's body.

But not when I look at him as only I can.

The smile in the polished bronze twisted up at one corner.

She raised her right hand and a girl came at once from the shadows with the wire-brush. She watched, the smile still upon her reddened lips, by the light of her oil lamp, as the slave began to bring out the fullness and lustre of her long, raven-black hair.

Yes, and maybe that too is my weapon for hers is only as the dry spelt way up in her own country, isn't it? I have seen it! Straight and thin and brittle!

After, she arose from her chair, her silken slip rustling, and the girl shrank away, bowing and cowering, back into the shadows. She extended her left arm toward her wardrobe and at once, two other slave-girls emerged from the darkness beyond her lamp and went to fetch her felt robe, which had been laid out upon her grand, gilt-framed bed. They grasped it and went to her and wrapped it reverently about her shoulders, the one pinning it with a polished, bone awl attached to a metal clip above her right breast, the other carefully arranging her hair down its back. The robe was a deep, rich, Royal Violet and glinted in the lamp-light.

She eyed herself approvingly in the bronze, saw how the robe brought out her piercing eyes. She turned her head. "Li-et," she growled deep within her throat, "My beautiful pet. Bring me my Crown."

Another girl, this one a mere child with sightless, clouded eyes, stepped noiselessly across the stone floor, bearing an emerald and ruby be-jeweled diadem upon a flaxen cushion. She went to her knees before her mistress and with small, steady hands held it up as high as her short arms could raise it.

Had-Ahah reached down and grasped the diadem and with her own hands placed it carefully upon her own brow.

In an instant, all of her slave-girls fell to their knees before her, hiding their faces in their hands upon the floor, and she smiled at herself in the mirror. *And now am I not truly the Queen of the World?* "And ready for your 'Occasion' too, My Husband," she whispered to herself, "and even for you, Vile Woman."

They came for her when the Sun was still an hour from its zenith, for that was the hour of the Magic Time, the Time of the Spirits of the World and of the Beyond, when the Great Father Cain had always called upon the All-Father, his Protector, to keep him from his enemies when he was still wandering, to remember the Sign that joined them and the Mark that linked them.

Absently, she reached with her left hand and clasped her right shoulder through her robe, next to the bone awl as Ohun, the Chamberlain, and two Guards of the Palace, escorted her through the stone hallways, past bronze stands alight with flame. Their footsteps echoed from the high, vaulted, stone ceilings.

They passed into the massive Main Chamber and the Queen raised her eyes to the high, distant roof of the room arrayed with the glittering Stars high above. *O Heavenly Lights, look down upon your servant, the Queen, and strengthen her hands for battle. May this day, she prevail against her adversary and win the King's undying devotion. May the one who opposes the rightful Queen stumble and bow the head before her so that she may crush it!*

Ohun approached the Great Doors of the Audience Chamber, which faced East, the Promise of the Great Father Cain, while she halted with the Guards beneath the high, vaulted Stars of the Beyond. She did not look up at them again but kept her gaze only upon the Doors. She knew that her eyes were sharp and alight and stiffened so that she stood tall, erect, and proud.

"I bring to the King, Had-Ahah, Queen of the East and Daughter of the Great Father!" announced Ohun in a deep, resounding voice that reverberated throughout the Main Chamber.

The four Guards at the Main Doors of the Audience Chamber bowed and then moved to slide aside the massive, iron bars, pulling and heaving the Great Doors open. Trembling with both adrenaline-fired fear and exultation, she saw four more Guards from within the inner sanctum, pushing at them as well. At last, with a powerful clang the Doors stood open before her.

Ohun stood aside before the doorway. Her escort stood arrayed about her. Ahead, within the Audience Chamber, she could spy the King seated upon his Throne, facing her. She felt them all looking to her, waiting. It was that ineffable moment - that moment for which she lived and was born.

Had-Ahah began to walk toward the Audience Chamber and her escort moved with her. Ohun lowered his eyes, bowing, as she passed, as did the Guards at the Doors, and then they were all behind her, including her escort and the four inner Guards, for she, alone, was permitted to be within the hallowed room with the King. She took two steps beyond the threshold and then paused.

The great doors swung to behind her with a resounding *boom*. Ahead, the King raised his sceptre in his right hand and lowered its rubied tip toward her. "Enter, My Queen!" he called out so that his voice echoed back from the high walls.

At once, she moved forward, striding purposefully, feeling her robe billowing behind her, and hearing the smart clicking of her ivory-heeled sandals upon the marble floor. She saw her husband clearly now, his dark gaze riveted upon her, both the familiar wonder and hunger visible in his eyes.

Yes, Heavenly Lights, for he is mine!

Slowly, deliberately, her eyes locked upon his, she mounted the first three of the five stone steps of the dais before the King's Throne, and then gracefully knelt upon the fourth, her robe whispering around her. Slowly and demurely lowering her gaze so that he might take in fully the *akhulah* upon her eyelids, she reached out and drew the head of his still-lowered sceptre toward her. Languidly, she bent and pressed it to her lips, sliding a brazen gaze up to him seated upon his Throne as she did so. "My King," she whispered.

He swallowed, looking down at her, his black eyes aglow but she could not tell the meaning of the strange glint that she suddenly perceived within them. "Oh, there is indeed a serpent within Kalneh," he rumbled deep in his throat then, his dark lips twisting lecherously, "and perhaps it is well that I have not ventured too near its scented den these three days. Hmm? I might well have been bitten." He barked out a rough laugh and then raised his sceptre again and thrust it within its narrow stand beside his throne. He reached down with his right hand and cupped her chin. Gently, but firmly, he raised it so that he looked straight into her eyes. She kept them steady and unblinking and proud and felt his thumb delicately brush her left cheek. "Who would think that something so comely could be so lethal," he said in a low, warning voice. "For I know of your jealousies." She felt her heart beating a tattoo within her chest but forced herself to keep her eyes upon his. The thumb moved to her painted, ruby lips and slowly brushed across them. She saw his gaze lower to her mouth. "Pleasure and a Sting," he said softly. "Honey and Poison. Hah!"

His arm shot out in a sweeping gesture to his right then. "Sit, My Queen!" he shouted, and now he was exultant suddenly, all warning and menace gone from him. "Sit and hear such news as your King will tell you. And perhaps there will even be some that all the World has not yet heard!"

At once, she arose and, drawing her robe tight about her shoulders and bowing, she retreated down the stone steps from before him. Then, turning, she saw that her own high Seat, of a level one step lower, had been drawn up hard aside his so that the arms of each would touch but for the Sceptre's stand between them. Erect and proud she mounted the steps to her own Throne and sat down upon its purple cushion and within its gilt arms, placing her slender, copper arms upon its armrests.

Then Ohun's voice barked out again from beyond the Chamber, but this time Had-Ahah heard it come from without the North entrance instead of the Main in the East. Automatically, she felt herself tense, her hands tightening upon the armrests of her throne. "I bring to the King, Azili-Lali, Queen of the North and Daughter of the Great Father!"

The smaller, Northern Doors began to open and Had-Ahah saw the Chamberlain stand aside beyond them.

And then *she* was there, standing within the doorway, her long, straight hair like the fields of flax that lay without the Towns in the far North of the Plain and beyond reaching down the front of her sheer, white gown, lined with the Royal Violet. With envy, Had-Ahah could not help but take in the woman's lovely and shapely form within that gown and, though she could not make out her Adversary's eyes from within the shining, milky-white skin of her face, she knew that they were filled with deceit and cunning. She felt herself tremble with rage.

"Aah!" exclaimed her husband, turning and regarding her rival, and reaching for his Sceptre. She watched him lower it toward the other. "Enter, My Queen," he called out to her and Had-Ahah heard a softness in his voice that had been gone from it these many days and even weeks when it had spoken to her. She shook upon her Seat.

The Rival strode across the floor, her sheer robe clinging to her body and flowing like a white wisp of cloud behind her, and now Had-Ahah could see the other's pale, grey eyes latched wickedly upon her husband's. And when she mounted the steps before the King's Throne and knelt down before him, whispering, "My King," suddenly he reached out and grasped her hand and lifted it to his lips!

It could not be borne and yet bear it she must. Had-Ahah growled deep in her throat, shuddering in rage, but remained silent. When her rival retreated from the Throne, she saw those pale, grey eyes flick to hers, challengingly, before the woman was mounting the three steps to her own Throne upon the King's left.

There was a moment of silence within the high chamber then, before the King took in a deep breath and said, "Now. Give me your hands. Both of you."

Silently, puzzled, her heart beating in her temples now, Had-Ahah obeyed and reached with her left hand toward him and clasped his large, roughened right one in hers. Both of their arms linked across the armrests of their thrones. He squeezed hers tightly. She saw him close his eyes.

What do you, My Husband?

"Yes," he murmured, "the time is right. The time is *now!*" He turned his head toward her and lifted her hand and kissed it and she was surprised by the tenderness of the caress upon her skin. "East," he said, softly, to her. Then turning to the other woman, she saw him do the same with her, except this time whispering, "North."

Her heart throbbed within her like a drum. *What is coming?*

"The World of the Great Father," he continued, raising his voice into the empty chamber, "in the forms and in the birthrights of my most beautiful Queens. Here, now, do you witness it, Great Father!" He raised his eyes to the high ceiling. "Here now do you see it, My Great Father Cain!"

Had-Ahah found herself shivering and staring up at the vault of the great room as if the Lights of the Heavens were peering down at her again. Her husband was still clutching her hand, almost painfully, and she could feel him shaking.

He brought her hand to his lips again along with *hers* but this time pulled on her arm as well so that she was compelled to turn toward him, shifting on her cushion. She saw her rival turn toward him also. "Queens of the East and of the North," he said, raising both of their hands in his and flourishing them, "hear my voice! Wives of Elah-Makah, harken to my words!" He turned to her. "Behold I now call thee 'Adah,'" he said, looking into her eyes, "For you have adorned your King with riches and splendour." He turned to the other. "And you shall be 'Zillah,' for you have overshadowed him with far off lands and realms.

"And behold! I have now not only the East and the North, My Queens, but this day I have reached out and grasped yet more!" He crammed her hand against his lips again, crushing her hand in his, and she almost cried out this time. "Today I have had a man killed! A man of the West! A man whose continued presence and existence had insulted me and my Realm and whose insolence had been a mockery to the Great Father himself!" He released her hand and she brought it, trembling, to her lap upon her silken slip and within her felt, Violet robe.

"I have killed the 'Ancient' of the Valley of Seth, the Enemy," whispered the King into the great room and Adah felt the hairs on her arms stand on end. "By my own command and by the might of my own Power, has this great deed been accomplished. With the help of my great Friends and Allies of the Grey Mountains was the Land of the Enemy this day breached! That great Enemy who dared to defy the Lord of the Plain and who had insulted the Great Father's name! If Cain is now avenged seven times on his brother, the Great Enemy, then *I* have been avenged *seventy*-seven times!"

He turned to her, exultant. "It is the greatest victory over our enemies since *she* was buried beneath the stones," he said in a low, tremulous voice. "And now I am no longer 'Elah-Makah,'" he shouted again, lifting his face once more to the high ceiling, "but now I am *LAMECH!* For I have made low the Line of Seth!"

Adah cried out in exultation along with him, taken up by the whelming tide of victory that washed over her and set her to shaking. She could *feel* the All-Father smiling down upon them, sitting there upon their anointed Thrones!

Ohun was at the open Doors at the Main Entrance again.

"All is prepared, My King!" he shouted. "As are our Esteemed Friends!"

Adah trembled upon her throne. *Is it the Special Occasion? A great spectacle, surely? A spectacle of Victory?*

She followed her King a step behind him and to his right, and the other woman did so upon the left. Ohun and Dalkus, the Captain of the Palace Guards and General of the King's Armies, led them through the Entrance of the Main Chamber of the Palace and they were flanked by a dozen soldiers. They headed out upon the grand, wide Avenue of the Moon, marching toward the East and the Plaza of the Sun in the Great City's very heart. The avenue was lined with soldiers and behind them, the Queen saw the crush of the crowds of the Great City, thronging and surging against the line of men. "The King! The King! Lamech! Lamech!" they cried, and she could see that they were raving, mad, in a state of ecstasy, at the sight of him, for he must have announced his new name, that name which he had bestowed upon himself, that name which signified his final victory over Seth!

She gasped and trembled as she walked, taking it all in, the energy, the Power of the faceless crowd, and she even heard her own name upon their lips: "Adah! Adah! The Queen! The Queen!" She was enraptured.

Upon the far side of the Plaza, stood the Ziggurat.

She raised her eyes up, up, up along the wide staircase that climbed its high, Western face as it drew steadily nearer and began to loom above them. Her eyes followed the stairs higher and higher to its very top and there, just at the limit of her sight, upon the Ziggurat's very pinnacle at the roof of the World, stood something.

Something.

She could not make out exactly what it was. She narrowed her eyes in the glare of the high, radiating Sun, shading them with her right hand, but could not see it clearly.

They climbed.

More soldiers stood to either side of the grand staircase of the great monument as they ascended. Her husband's entire, vast army, she knew, surrounded the City, lining its every, grand boulevard. She could almost not climb for the shaking that had taken her over. It was the very splendour of his Power, his might on display for all the World to witness. No less! She found herself staring, open-mouthed up, up, up to the very summit of the stone steps. And the Object that stood there.

They reached the roof of the world and Adah felt the wind stir her robe about her legs. Her long hair stirred about her shoulders and beneath her diadem. The wind was from the East, from the gloomy, mist-enshrouded Grey Mountains and she cast her gaze quickly toward them.

Her shaking was deep, deep in her bones, for now she saw clearly what else stood atop the height of the World with them. The Object, itself, was covered from top to bottom with a shroud like to that which clothed those Mountains. And arrayed around it, stood.....

Eneph!

What are they doing here?

Four of them there were and they stood huge and powerful around the Object from its Southern side around to its Northern, opposite to the grand stair and facing toward them. Adah saw that they wore grey, linen *shendyts* about their waists, which reached down to their knees and which seemed to shimmer and shift in the light of the high Sun whenever they moved. Each grasped the shaft of an enormous spear that was twice the height of a man. The first, and tallest, of them, who stood at the South of the Ziggurat's high platform, alone wore also a robe about his high, massive shoulders and bore no weapon of any kind that she could behold.

Their long, grey hair was tied behind their backs with threads of grey fabric so thick they were like ropes. And their liquid eyes gleamed at them from their brows In colours of amber and blue and green. The first one's shone out the colour of bright blood and she gasped and looked away from them once she had seen them.

She trembled, not long meeting each of their gazes and for a moment they were all still. The tumult of the crowds washed up toward them from far below in ripples of sound.

At last the King turned and looked down upon the Square and the people surging and milling below.

He raised his Sceptre high in the air and the din of the crowd gradually subsided.

Slowly he turned back and faced the Object and the *Eneph*.

Shrugging out of his outer robe, satin and Violet, he draped it over his left arm. Adah, beholding his bared Mark upon his right arm, hastened to imitate him, bearing her own. The other did so as well.

Lamech took two steps toward the first *Eneph* and she saw that they met one another's eyes. "Seer," said the King, "I behold the Realm of My Esteemed Friends and Allies, shrouded above the World, far in the East, and gazing out over the Earth, over the land of the Enemy of My Great Father Cain." He extended his right hand toward the robed *Eneph*.

"Lamech, Son of Cain," rumbled the *Eneph,* the one her husband had called 'Seer,' in a harsh, thick tongue that she could barely understand, "I behold the Mark of your Great Father, and acknowledge his reverence for the All-Father himself. I acknowledge the Son of Cain's claim to the Realms of Men, to his Lordship of all Human Domains."

The Queen watched as the Seer of the *Eneph* reached out his massive arm and clasped the right arm of Lamech, King of the World.

"A new Dawn," said Lamech, then, "and now let nothing stand in the way of the Mountains and of the Plain. For is not now all of the Earth before us?"

The Seer released his arm and then, with a sweep of his massive hand, gestured out toward the West. "I See the Enemies of Cain fall before the might of his son, even those who have until now lived in the West, beyond his reach. I See a great cataclysm befalling all who oppose him and which shall swallow up all their lands like a mighty Cleansing hand. I See the very Earth itself renewed without our Enemies."

The King turned to the West and gazed out toward it, beyond the City and the Plain, and the wind from the East stirred his hair about his brow, beneath his Crown. Adah was conscious of her heart racing in her chest as if it would burst clean out of it.

"Now let us show our Enemies to *Him,*" he said, "He who has given us the final victory! He who will purge the World of Seth!"

They went and stood, the King and the Seer, each at the side of the Object, grasping its shroud in their hands.

With a great pull, It was bared at last.

"HAIL THE ALL-FATHER!"

Adah, Queen of the World, fell to her knees upon the Ziggurat's stone roof and buried her face inside her hands, shuddering and whimpering with fear. She tried not to look at it again but saw it still within her mind's eye, imprinted there as if it would never fade away.

A great, black Serpent, reared up as if to strike, crowned, with ruby eyes.

Facing towards the West.

V

"Whoah, whoah!" called out Ajah-Phethah.

All of the servants and pack animals came to a halt next to the High River, as they had taken to calling this one. He was aware that Asheh-Mah was suddenly beside him, no doubt due to seeing Artuah and the scouts returning from up ahead. Ajah-Phethah wiped his wet brow with his cloak sleeve. It was nigh on midday of the second since they had first seen and stepped out into this new high valley and the day after the one in which Father and the old servant had left them to scrabble through the dry brush across it for who knew where. *A hike to the foothills in the North, he had called it - or some such - and then they would catch us up.* It had made no sense to him then and made no sense to him now. And yet Father could be stubborn when the mood struck him. He sighed, waiting as the men drew closer.

Artuah held his wooden bow in his hand and his hide quiver full of arrows was slung over his shoulder. His ram's horn was hooked into his hide belt. "Masters," he said, "not a hundred paces on the High River bends towards the North and passes through a low trough of rock. Altes found a cave in the Eastern side there - on our side. There is a shallow place after the turn of the river not unlike the Wash within the Valley of Seth where the far side may be gained. I sent two men across there and they have told me that out across the grass field that lies hard by there, there is to be found nothing but tall, dark trees barring the way farther. They did not enter them. Here upon this side of the River beyond the rocky trough it becomes narrower and leads up high into the foothills that climb into the West. Only one or two men at most must needs ascend beyond that point and that would be a right climb indeed! I think we have come to the end of this new Valley."

Ajah-Phethah turned to his brother. "What do you think? Shall we set up and wait for Father?"

Asheh-Mah gave out a grunt. "There's no sense traipsing up and down and all around." He pointed up across the River to their left toward the near foothills and the farther mountains in the South that had been with them since they had emerged from the narrow Valley of Stone two days ago. "Nothing there and to the North more mountains across the grasses such as Father and the old servant headed for. Now based on what Artuah is telling us there are yet more mountains in *front* of us, along with this forest! If Father was looking for a great 'Source' to this 'High' River, then I'm afraid he'll be sorely disappointed. Unless he wants to take A-Phthah on another hike when he gets here." He pointed straight ahead to the West.

Ajah-Phethah nodded, frowning. "I suppose you're right," he mumbled, "but don't you get the feeling that we're missing something - something that's right in plain sight? Maybe even at our very feet?"

"What do you mean?"

"I mean - " and Ajah-Phethah turned and strode away from the River out across the valley for a space, "that, for one thing, this grass here is different from the grass we've been trampling on ever since we arrived up here."

Asheh-Mah let out a loud laugh. "You've gotten too much sun, Brother," he called out to him. "Your wits are addled with the heat and the thinner air."

Ajah-Phethah motioned at him, impatiently. "Just come here. See for yourself what I mean."

Shaking his head, Asheh-Mah headed out across the grass to join him.

"Now," said his brother, "look down here and then up along the ground back toward the East where we've come. Do you notice anything?"

Asheh-Mah clicked his teeth in exasperation but looked down. The wind freshened suddenly and blew through the yellow stalks. He shivered. *Is that a voice in the air?*

[Seeeeeeee......]

He followed with his eyes the bowing heads of grass back down the valley.

It was as if something fell from his eyes.

"Wait a minute," he murmured. "Wait!" He scuffed at the dry ground with the bone soles of his tough, hide sandals. "The ground here is disturbed and eroded," he whispered. He looked up toward the East and pointed. "The grass we've seen all this way is taller and more slender. *This grass - "* He thrust his finger down at his feet " - is shorter and 'rougher.'" He stared at his brother.

"A crop field," they said, together.

They let the realization sink in.

"Someone," said Ajah-Phethah, in a low voice, "harvested grain here. Barley. Maybe millet too." His voice was shaking and his eyes met Asheh-Mah's. "But a long time ago. Just look at it. It's been fallow for years."

"Not just years, Brother," whispered Asheh-Mah, shaking his head. "Centuries." He raised his hands up at his sides, imploringly, and shook them. "But *who?*"

Ajah-Phethah swallowed. "I think we'd better set up Camp," he said, dryly.

Asheh-Mah nodded and then turned away. Striding back to the rest of the group gathered near the river, he shouted, "Set up Camp! We'll await the Master here."

As the rest of the group began to bustle and break out the tents and supplies, Ajah-Phethah remained where he was, looking out once more at the blowing grasses whispering all around him. "And I think I want to see this 'cave' too," he murmured to himself.

It was dark inside, even though Ajah-Phethah had wisely chosen the late afternoon to enter. The cave was surprisingly deep into the rock of the river-bed and its 'door' he noticed faced exactly toward the lowering sun. There was a gap out to the West between where the Southern and Northern lines of the Mountains seemed to draw almost nigh to each other and the sun was slowly falling into it. Depressions in the rock had risen to the cave's mouth and upon the threshold there was a wide, flat stone. As soon as he had beheld them, he had not been able to shake the notion that the depressions were stairs and that the flat stone was a 'bench.' The shiny, worn surfaces of each seemed to bespeak long years of treading feet and even of sitting bottoms.

Ajah-Phethah gave a sniff. He and Artuah and one other of the scouting men were cautiously probing the interior. *Dank, yet…..* He crouched down and swept the floor of the cave with his open palm. Dust clung to it. Absently, he wiped his hands together. "Dry," he said aloud. He looked up. "If anyone was here, they are long gone."

"Master," spoke up Artuah, then, and his voice echoed eerily around them from the walls of rock. Ajah-Phethah shivered. The archer was standing in the far corner and Ajah-Phethah could scarcely make him out. "See here." He pointed to something nearby.

Frowning, Ajah-Phethah got up and went over to him.

"A jar of stone," Artuah murmured.

Ajah-Phethah could see it now. Of a height with his waist, it was almost as big around as his arms would reach if he had a mind to carry it. Eagerly, he got down and reached inside it. Slowly withdrawing his hand, he let the contents of the jar slip, coolly, through his fingers.

"Dust," he said to no-one in particular. "And that's all they are now too - whoever they were."

"Seth," said Artuah, suddenly, and Ajah-Phethah jerked toward him, feeling the little hairs on his skin rise up. "I just know it was. Master….. what if the Great Father himself lived here? Long before he came to his Valley. What if *he himself* used this jar?"

Ajah-Phethah stood erect at once. He felt his heart throbbing in his temples. "We must find Asheh-Mah and return to the Camp," he said and quickly turning he left the dark place.

He found his brother out across the field beyond the fording place where the River turned. He was standing before the line of tall trees that Artuah had mentioned.

"Nothing like them in the Valley of Seth," said Asheh-Mah, staring up at them, as Ajah-Phethah approached. "Have you ever seen their like?"

Ajah-Phethah stood silently, looking up at the trees. Dense they were and taller by far than any within the Valley of Seth, it was True; they towered above them, standing there in the waning afternoon. The sun was well behind them now and even the wind was stilled for no breath passed through their dark hulks. Ajah-Phethah could see the roughness of their bark as if they bore years uncounted upon them, and there was a stillness so deep and utter amongst them that it made him shudder in his sandals to listen to it.

"I mislike them," he whispered, not wanting even to raise his voice around them. *They know we're here. They're listening to us.* "It's like they're guarding something, barring our way." He turned to his brother. "Perhaps Father and A-Phthah will be rejoining us tomorrow."

Asheh-Mah also stood rooted at the edge of the forest, staring into its dim silence. Slowly, he nodded. "Yes," he said, in a low voice. "Let's head back to Camp. I do not want to be here when it is full dark."

Anoh-Ah grasped a handful of twigs and a bigger branch and half-rose and threw them onto the fire. At once, the flames leapt up. It had been burning lower within the ring of stones that he and A-Phthah had set up just before sunset and he was grateful that it had caught with the flint and the metal. Night was fast approaching and up here the air was thinner and a good deal colder even than in the High Valley.

He had already learned much about how sheltered the Line of Seth had been back in Seth's beautiful and protected Valley far behind and below.

And now You are leading us all out and into the greater, harder World, Abba Father - a World that no longer cares for Good or for the Great Father and his Faith. Or even for You. You are leading us out to a great Reckoning. I feel it. I know it. Lead on!

He shivered, sitting back down and watching the flames. He drew his cloak tighter about himself.

Beyond the fire-light stood a Man.

He felt his heart leap into his throat but at once found himself calling out into the night air in a surprisingly steady voice, "Come and join us, Friend."

The man was cloaked and hooded in shadow. No face could Anoh-Ah discern within the folds of his hood even though the fire was high. Indeed its flickering light seemed to pass right over the Man, as if he were a part of the night itself.

"I thank you for your offer," the Stranger said, presently, and his voice was kind, yet to the man seated before the fire, it did not seem to issue from the hood but from the very air all around them. "For not all who sit by a fire in these Present Days welcome me."

Anoh-Ah found that his heart was throbbing, pulsing through every sinew of his body. He darted his eyes to his trusted servant - to

A-Phthah - and found him asleep beside the fire, slumped over on his own stone seat.

Now when did he drift off? A fine time to do it!

The Stranger moved to sit upon A-Phthah's far side so that he and Anoh-Ah were at right angles to one another before the fire. Anoh-Ah saw that he carried in his hand a walking stick that was moon-silver and which seemed to shimmer with its own light. Or was it the hand that held it that did so? "Oh, do not worry about this one," said the Man, sitting with a sigh, and indicating A-Phthah. "He is well known and has his own path to walk."

Anoh-Ah, heart still fluttering, watched the other place his stick carefully against the ring of stones beside him.

"Do you live nearby, Sir?" he said, faintly.

"I?" said the Stranger and he turned his hood slightly toward him. He chuckled softly and then turned to look out over his shoulder at the High Valley away below them and Anoh-Ah turned to look as well. "Indeed, I have lived here long. The Mountains, the Grasses, the River - I know them well." And then, though the night had fallen and it was full dark, yet as the Man named each, Anoh-Ah saw first the mountains and then the grasses and then the river brighten slightly as if they were bathed in a translucent light and then were dimmed once more. He gasped.

The hood turned fully toward him now though still no face was visible within. "And the Animals," spoke the voice from the air again, "Ah! Beautiful, they were! For they too were here. Yes! For a time. The Fish first, and then the Birds. Then all of the others that move upon the ground. I have travelled far throughout the world, seeking after them and watching over them, for they have spread far and wide since that day." He sighed again. "The day in which all things changed. And yet - " The hood lowered slightly " - in spite of the beauty of Mountain or Grass or River or Animal, it is the very Truth that it is in Man and Woman that I find my greatest joy." The hood lifted. "Oh, yes. To walk with them, to hear their voices. To feel their faces and hearts turned toward me in Love. Aaah! Now *that* there is nothing like - especially since that day!"

A sublime moment thrilled the night air around Anoh-Ah for an instant and then the Stranger was quiet for a long time while Anoh-Ah watched him in fascination.

Finally, he said, "That is why I thank you."

The fire hissed and crackled and Anoh-Ah turned to watch the flames lick hungrily into the night air.

All at once, a great drowsiness filled him…..

VI

He stood in darkness and there was not a sound. He was afraid.

Presently, he saw a mist. It lay heavily all around him, as a blanket of wool, and he held up his hands as if to ward it off, to push it away. He strained his eyes, trying to see through it.

Then it was rent aside and at once, grass grew beneath his feet, thrusting up from the ground, green and long and lush. A wind came and trees bent over him suddenly, their leaves, both broad and thin, rustling and fluttering, their boughs heavy-laden with fruit. He looked around at them and beheld the fruit in great variety and abundance. Then, above the crowns of the trees, he saw stars shining down brightly upon him from a vast, inky sky. He saw their splendour now in greater magnitude, now in lesser. And a bright, silver moon shone down from among them, limning his arms in a ghostly light. Then there came to his ears a rushing sound.

He stood at a river's flowing, churning side and now the sun was shining down upon its foaming crests. It was vast and wide and ceaseless and he felt its power and greatness welling up from the ground itself. Suddenly, a Fish leapt up high into the air with a spiny tail and diaphanous fins! Soundlessly, he laughed at it in delight. Then another leapt up! And another! Each one was different in colour and vividness. Above, in the sky,

Birds came, great birds with wide wings of red and blue and white and brown and black, calling and swooping and diving. Their cries pierced him and their songs touched him in a way that made him feel as if he had always been happy, always been full of joy, always been with *them* and they with him! Then a cry behind him came and he whirled and beheld a Tiger stalking toward him, followed by its mate and two cubs. Bounding from the trees behind them came a Deer, a great buck, with a massive rack of antlers. With him too came his mate and their young. Rabbits and Squirrels and even Monkeys burst forth from warrens and the trees standing all about, and yet others, creatures that he had never before seen! Each of them scampered and scrambled and crept and leapt around him so that he felt his head spin with the sheer movement of them.

With joy, he watched all and everything around him for a long, long time and he knew nothing else.

Then there came another sound upon the air.

He paused and listened.

It was New.

Curious, he followed the sound, passing from River and through Trees and Grass, and hearing the Animals' cries grow fainter behind him.

Ahead, there was a rise and he climbed it and when he had reached the top he looked down. There, below, was a Man and a Woman.

VII

They knelt at the foot of the rise, facing away from him.

He saw at once that they were naked. And yet, as he beheld them, he knew that it was their only natural state. There could be no other, for they were not *made* for another. Young they were, very young, and beautiful. They were more beautiful than any human beings that he had ever before seen and their naked bodies seemed to shine before his eyes. He stared at them in awe and wonder. They were holding each other's hands and speaking softly to one another. And it was their voices that he had heard on the air.

"Ashah-Inah," said the man, linking his fingers with the woman's. "Atoh-Vah."

"Achah-Zakah," said the woman, clasping her hands in the man's. "Atoh-Vah."

Then he saw, beyond them, a basket of wicker upon the ground and it was filled to bursting and piled high with lush fruit and vivid vegetables the likes of which he had never before seen. He did not even know the names of them. Then the Stranger stood over them!

Only.....it was not the Stranger.

He gave a start. None of them had noticed him standing there above them and watching them and, fascinated, he continued to watch silently as the Figure stepped closer to the Man and the Woman and held out his hands to them, kneeling there upon the ground. Heart bursting, he saw the Man and the Woman slip theirs, shyly and gently, into his. *No, he is not a Stranger to THEM. They know him! They love him!*

And he them.

The Stranger was their Friend.

It was the Friend, therefore, who lifted up the Man and the Woman from the ground and passed on through the trees with them.

He was left alone. Except for another sound, soft, rustling, whispering.

Whirling, he thought to himself that he had seen something flicker out of sight at the bottom of the rise below him. He turned and descended, in the opposite direction to which the three had gone.

He followed after the flicker, the whisper, followed after its soft murmuring on the air. The wood grew thicker around him and the sunlight through the branches dwindled.

Before him stood a tree, huge and dark. An Oak.

He looked high up to its lofty crown and all at once a shiver stole through him. The forest became cold. Lowering his eyes to the ground he saw that the tree's roots had grown out of the ground on one side like giant, twisted, gnarled fingers. Beyond and within them, there was a thick blackness.

Creeping closer to this place, he heard the soft whisper again. Out of the hole in the roots it came and as he heard it this time, he shuddered to his very soul.

"Death," it hissed. "Death."

With a cry, he sat before the fire again and the wind howled around him, whipping the flames upward in a great whirlwind. Terrified, he cried out again but his voice was caught up in the very vortex of flame. A-Phthah had disappeared. The Stranger was gone.

Overhead, the sky was black for the stars had vanished. Clouds, dark and churning, covered the sky.

Wait! Come back! He screamed the words but there was no sound.

The wind ceased.

The fire died and went out.

Darkness again.

Yet not quite, for now the sky above was streaked with blood. He stood upon dully gleaming grass at the foot of two tall Trees. Beside him, in the gloaming, two figures writhed upon the ground.

One of them spoke - a groan of anguish and anger: "Get up! We've got to get out of here!" He saw that it was a man, with pinched, pallid face and sunken eyes.

The other, a thin, frail, woman, was groaning and shaking and her cries were of deep despair. "No!" she wailed upon the grass. "Come back! Fill me again! Don't leave me alone!"

He felt his heart sear like a hot brand from the newly-dead fire as he saw them and heard their pain-drenched voices. He fell to his knees and the ground around him was wet with leaves and twigs. Surrounding him was a forest of tall, utterly dark trees.

It was raining now and overhead, far, far above the thick canopy, he could hear it beating down. Thunder rumbled through the very ground beneath him and flashes of lightning gashed bolts of dazzling light through the darkness.

He staggered to his feet and began to grope through the thick wood with his hands outstretched before his face. Then, stumbling down into a sunken clearing, a flash of lightning revealed two figures crouched nearby. He jerked his head toward them.

They were bent over, gasping, their hands upon their knees. Then one was pointing toward him and he wanted to turn and flee, to hide! Yet his feet were stuck to the ground and he could not. He saw the second figure take two steps toward him and then stop.

Behind him, the first one rose up like a shadow, looming, and another lightning-flash revealed a sharpened rock in his hand! It was raised high.

He tried to cry out, to warn the other, but the stone fell like a bolt from the sky before he could open his mouth.

The cry died in his throat.

He was in the air now. High, high above the ground. He was flying! It was night and he soared through the dark, feeling a tempest of wind buffeting him from every direction. Below, far, far below the ground moved with rivers of flame. Villages burned, cities were razed. Bodies of men, women, and children lay scattered across the ground, hacked, slain. He saw that they were old, young, black, white, bronze, olive.

The Plain was on fire and armies of men marched across it, led by dark, shrouded kings.

He flew on. Ahead were Mountains now, strange and jagged. It was still dark but for the bloody glow upon the Plain, and now the peaks rising up before him gleamed grey in the night. He felt a stab of fear but flew on, diving now between two out-thrusting spurs of the nearest mountain.

Down he went, down, down, down so that he shot through a chasm rent like a black mouth between the shoulders of rock.

A stifling heat engulfed him as he flew and now there were fires kindled in holes in the rock. Great, huge figures gathered, powerful bodies sweating, milling, dancing. Their voices were like thunder and they chanted in dread voices. Men and animals were there, chained and wailing in anguish and pain.

There was an Idol. In the deepest pit, surrounded by flames it stood. A gigantic figure of a Serpent, coiling to strike. Its eyes shone with the fire that burned all around it, fire that never died and was never satisfied. Before it, upon a slab of blackened stone stained Crimson, writhed a naked, wretched, wailing man…..

The fire was crackling, sending up sparks into the clear, cold, night air. The stars were shining down, bright as diamonds.

He was doubled over on his knees, shaking and ill, retching upon the grass before the fire.

"Ah!" cried a piercing voice and it was drenched in agony. "Do you hear it?"

Still shaking, Anoh-Ah looked up slowly.

The Stranger sat before the fire once more, his hood turned toward the flames. "Innocence lost," said his voice from the air, "Hope withered. Love abandoned." The hood moved slowly toward him. "Life destroyed. Blood spilt. Creation maimed."

Anoh-Ah stared back at him, unable to speak.

"The blood of the heaps of all of the slain cries out to me," said the Stranger. "Ceaselessly. Day after day it screams its agonies in my ear. For the Life of all that Lives is within the Blood. And now this world grieves me, for it has shed so much of it. So much! It pierces my heart. And I wish that it had never been."

Fire like living flames surged through Anoh-Ah at these words. "What…..what is to be done?" he gasped. "How can it be made…..*right?*"

The Stranger looked at him fully now and his unseen eyes glinted in the fire-light. Anoh-Ah saw him lift a long finger to the front of his hood. "Shhhhh," he whispered. "Hush now. Be still. Shall I not reveal to you - you who almost alone upon this Fallen Earth walks before me with a True heart - what I am about to do? And shall not all who come hereafter speak of it to their children for all generations?"

Anoh-Ah felt held fast as if by a great hand. Trembling, he remained on his knees before the fire; before the Man.

"You are Noah," said the Stranger.

Anoh-Ah, NOAH, felt a shiver run through him.

"I tell you that even in this world of toil and war, you shall yet know rest and peace upon it. You shall see these days renewed, days of new Hope. Behold, I have blessed thee."

Noah felt warm tears slide down his cheeks.

The finger lowered and pointed at him.

"Your wife, I name Emzara, for she shall be the foremother of one who shall bear my further Promise. Your sons are Shem - for he shall bear the name of my People; Japheth - for he shall enlarge them; and Ham - for he shall burn new paths and spread out in the days afterward. When it is finished."

Noah trembled. "Finished," he whispered.

The Stranger stood up. He reached out his hand. "Take hold of my cloak," he said.

With a shaking hand, Noah reached out and grasped its sleeve.

In an instant, an eternity, he saw. He saw *everything!*

VIII

"Let me have a look at you."

Tentatively, Neltamuk stepped farther into her Mistress's room. The sheer ochre hangings fell back into place behind her, cutting her off from her parents, whom she knew were standing, humbly, behind her in the centre part of the tent, near the hearth and beneath the great, open hole in its roof.

"Please," said the Mistress, pointing toward the doorway, "have your parents come in as well. I wish to acknowledge them."

Neltamuk turned. "Father, Mother, come in. The Mistress wants to see you."

After a few moments, the hangings were moved aside again and, even more tentatively, the girl's parents stepped quietly into the room.

The Mistress smiled and her dark eyes glinted. "Excellent," she said, looking from face to face. *"Abba Father* be praised."

All three visitors to her room bowed their heads and repeated the words in quiet murmurs.

Emzara - for that was her name now; she had been shown it last night in Dream - stood up from her couch. She was arrayed this morning in her ochre wrap and robe and she stepped toward the girl, raising her hands. "I greet you as a mother," she said to the girl, "and call you Daughter."

Neltamuk gasped and at once lowered her eyes. She began to tremble.

"Ah!" said the Mistress. "When we are alone or with your good-sisters, the other wives of my sons, you shall look me in the eyes. For you are now, or will be when the Master arrives, a Daughter of Seth as well as of Azura. Yes? Will you not also give birth to the Great Father's sons?"

Neltamuk looked up, blew out a low breath, nodded.

In her hand, Emzara held a scarf of ochre and this she raised up and tied about the girl's neck. It was the sign of the Great Father.

The old woman standing nearby let out a gasping sob and the old man drew her tightly to him.

Behind them, the hangings were again drawn aside.

"Mistress," spoke the head of a servant-girl hovering in the doorway, "your daughters are without."

"Good!" said Emzara and she raised her hands toward the door. "Let them come, that we may greet them."

The servant withdrew and then two more women entered the room, each bearing a scarf, wrap, and robe of ochre.

The older couple, the girl's parents, hastened away into a corner of the room, bowing while Neltamuk, herself, turned toward the newcomers timidly.

"My good-daughters," said the Mistress, still with her arms held out toward them as if in supplication, "I would have you greet one another as sisters before my eyes."

The two women turned toward Neltamuk. The first held her arms straight down at her sides, palms open and facing outward. Then bending them at the elbows, she crossed them over her chest. "I am Sedeqe, wife of Shem, Son of the Master," she said. Neltamuk saw that she was fair-haired and fair-skinned. "My Family dwells far away to the North of the Plain. Today, I call you Sister."

"I am Hadata," said the second, laying her arms straight at her sides and then folding them across her chest also. She had the complexion of copper and with hair of brown with red streaks winding through it, even as the grey wound its way through the Mistress's black. "Wife of Japheth, from far in the East, from even beyond the Grey Mountains. Today, I call you Sister."

Still trembling, Neltamuk imitated their gestures. She told them her name and from where her family had come and called them 'Sister' too.

And then she saw it. *What Akad-Amon said. The Ending and the Beginning!*

They were, none of them, the wives of the Master's sons, from the West, from out of Seth - unless it were long, long years uncounted and from the Great Father himself!

We have been brought together again by Abba Father from the far ends of the world! North, East, South! White, Copper, Black!

She shivered now so that her whole body shook.

The Mistress frowned. "Neltamuk? Daughter? Is everything all right?"

Startled, the girl turned towards her new mother. "Yes," she whispered, "everything is all right. Everything is more than all right. We just have to trust *HIM!*"

"Trust Him," repeated Emzara, quietly. She smiled. "That is Truth. I have a wise daughter."

She reached out and drew them all, her good-daughters, to herself and embraced them tightly.

Outside, to the South and East of the small cluster of the Family tents that lay near to the bank of the River, Ham stood with the two Scribes. The one bore the official tally of the Fruit of all of the trees in the Valley and the Vegetables of the ground upon his clay slate and the other that of the Grains of the fields to the South.

"Yes, that is fine," he told the first. "The men will continue to bring them in." He gestured toward the broad, well-worn path that led on into the woods to the North along the River-bank. "I have told them that they must work until nightfall. Everything - as much as can be dug and picked and hauled - without pause until the darkness. All must be taken in and packed." He lowered his voice and all but whispered into the man's ear, "It is all by *his* instructions. You understand? Something…..hmmmm….. Time is of the essence."

"I quite understand, Master," replied the Scribe. He made a final etching upon the slate with his wedge-shaped reed and then bowing and tucking both under his arm, he went away, briskly, and resumed his oversight of the teams of men and mules trundling out of the woods with their heavily-laden carts.

After a similar conversation with the second official of the Household, who hastened away to the South and to the long line of carts filled with Grains, Ham suddenly turned and looked about him. "Akad-Amon?" he called. *Where has the Ancient got to?*

He drew his ochre-trimmed, white robe more tightly about himself and shuddered.

What was it he said? Why the Fruit and Vegetables and Grains had to come in and be packed in haste? Why we will have to leave the Valley?

The Ending.

And the Beginning?

He looked up at the slate, grey sky.

Everything was still. As if the world were holding its breath.

There had been no blight in the crops, no insect-sign of any kind amongst them.

There had been strange behaviour amongst the Birds; many had been seen to be leaving the Valley also. Flying West in great tumult and distress. The Ibis, especially, the great, honoured Birds of the South, had taken wing toward the falling sun.

I do not understand it all, A-Abba Father. He took in a deep breath; tried to still his fear. Fear, Father had told him once, was the Faith-Killer. It gave the Enemy a foothold in the heart - in the Valley of one's soul.

He did not always understand his father's words. Nor his mother's.

I will do better, Abba Father. I promise!

He jumped, gasping. "Akad-Amon!" he exclaimed. "I did not see you come."

"Hmph," grunted the old man, standing behind him upon the path. "Nor leave." He reached out and chucked his great-grandson on the shoulder with a bony hand. "I've watched you, Young Master. I observe." He tapped the side of his old head. "I see more than people know or give me credit for. Yes? Which is why I tell you to observe more for yourself. One day, *you* will be 'Master' - Master in your own right. Master in your own Family. Master in your own Land. A land Renewed. Here and now, you have a Betrothed. There and then, you will have a Family and a new Beginning. But first - " and he pointed a crooked finger up into the younger man's wide-eyed, startled face " - you will have an 'Ending.'"

Ham swallowed, dryly.

"Now, follow me." Abruptly, the Ancient turned and Ham noticed that he was animated with a fervent energy; his old body was less stooped. Wordless, he followed.

Together, they hiked South along the path and soon left the River and began to meander amongst the outliers of the woods. They took a smaller branch that led East, right up to the side of the Valley itself. Here, they had to climb and the old man stabbed the heel of his staff into the ground as they went. Soon they were huffing and Ham felt a sheen of sweat begin to stand out all over his body. He marvelled at the old man's endurance. The trees here were sparser but again, he noticed that the woods, everything around them, was eerily still. It was as if no creature nor bird was anywhere around them, nor had ever been.

He shivered.

They reached a shelf of rock in the side of the Valley which looked far out over the River to North, West, and South and Ham turned to take it all in. He gasped, holding his heaving side.

"You feel it, don't you?" breathed Akad-Amon.

Ham ripped his eyes from the world around them and fastened them upon the old face, the tired eyes.

The old man lifted his staff and pointed its tip at the sky. "Behold," he said, gaspingly, "The Sun is dimmed, the blue of the Sky has gone grey."

Ham lifted his gaze to the heavens. *"Abba Father* save us," he whispered, seeing.

In the West, just above the lip of the Valley, for the foothills had tapered off here and the River was on its way into the far South, where the great grain-fields lay, he saw a faint shimmering - like a vapour rising up from the Earth. He pointed. "And what is *that?"* he said, his voice no more than a gasp.

The old man looked where he pointed and gave out a great sigh. "Behold, thou art Methuselah," he rasped, his eyes fixed upon the shimmering in the West, "and I will yet show you where you must hurl your javelin. At your enemy's very feet! Before the Ending."

Ham stood still. He did not speak. The strange vapour, haze, shimmering in the West, whatever it was, continued to ensnare his gaze.

"I see the Sun disappear and the Stars vanish," intoned the old man - Methuselah, "I see the River and the Valley and the foothills washed away. And they are no more."

Tears sprang into the ancient eyes, those eyes that had seen far more than Ham could possibly imagine. The old, lined face turned toward him.

"The Ending is what you see," whispered Methuselah. His hand came up slowly and that single, gnarled finger pointed to the West. "The Birds and the tiny creatures that scurry upon the ground sense what we do not. More will yet. The dimness will increase until there is only darkness left. The sun will fail and the moon fall dark. The Earth itself will be.…..broken."

Ham gaped at him.

"Then, at the last, there will be left only *Abba Father* and those whom He has chosen." Methuselah's gaze as it held the younger man's was pure serenity despite the words of calamity that fell from his lips. "Only they will see the Light return. Only they."

IX

He sat within his tent, brooding.

Whether this one is in league with Seth or no makes no difference. All that he has, his family, his slaves, his animals, his land, his possessions - all must be destroyed. The infection and taint of rebellion, of treachery must be eradicated so that all of the other Towns will see it and tremble.

He curled his fist around his copper goblet.

And they will. But first, his Town must be levelled, mustn't it? He nodded. *It must be made to burn, to become a heap of cinders and rubble and ash to serve as an example of what happens to acts of defiance. And then he will be offered up in the usual way, the proven way.*

The Great Father must be honoured and the All-Father appeased.

Outside, a stiff breeze stirred the tent; the thick, hide walls billowing out and then in again, like a great bellows.

He was aware of the movement, sensed a change in the wind. A cold breath entered the tent and reached up under his robe with icy fingers. *By Cain, have I never felt a Cold like this outside of the Mountains before! It portends something.*

My victory? Or.....?

Vexed, and in sudden doubt, he shot to his feet, knocking over his small, austere, leather-covered chair.

Then Dalkus was standing in the doorway, holding apart the heavy, hide flaps.

"My King," he said, in a low voice that carried just above the sighing of the wind outside, "The….. Seer…..awaits you without."

Lamech, his heart fluttering and sweat now standing out on his skin, swallowed. *I must master myself! Am I not King of all?*

Composing himself, he drew his robe tighter about his shoulders. "I will go to him," he told his general, "for he will not willingly intrude upon my space. He is…..sensible like that."

More like he will not defile himself with the things of Men and is most anxious to begin the slaughter.

The expression upon Dalkus's countenance told him that the high officer was thinking the same thing - but wisely refusing to give it voice.

He found his great Ally standing with a dozen of his number, facing East.

Always facing those impenetrable Mountains of theirs. Accursed they are. If the Great Father ever set foot there, he never told my Fathers of it. I have never been able to take my Army thence. Only far down to the Great Sea or up, up far into the Northern wastes.

"The sky is soon the colour of Blood and Fire, O King," the Seer's giant voice swelled around him, jolting him out of his reverie. "What you have come to do must be done at once." The great, swimming, liquid-flame eyes turned toward him.

Lamech trembled and looked out to the East as well and felt that ice-breeze push at him from behind. There was a line of bruised pink and purple on the horizon. He steeled himself and let the old adrenaline begin to wash over him. "Time indeed," he growled. "Let it be done, Great Friend." He darted his eyes to the other's. "Let the two of us be now as one. Let our fists, in this hour, together smash our Enemies and show no Mercy."

The other *Eneph,* those who stood like dark towers around the Seer, laughed in fell voices at this and the Seer raised a clenched fist larger than a man's head into the air. At once, the other giants, some dozen of them turned away and Lamech saw that they were joined now by another dozen, each bearing a huge, burning torch - and the lead of a like number of their Creatures, which Lamech had never before seen up close and which had countenances and statures so terrifying that he was compelled to step back from them as they approached. He could see the riders' enormous spears strapped to their flanks.

But for their size, they would be horses. The beasts were greater and larger than the wild aurochs that he had at times seen in the High Plain when he was campaigning there. Purest black they were and, in the light of the many torches, he was stunned to see giant, folded, wings at their flanks! They seemed to let the glow of the flames pass right through them, however, as if they were translucent rather and of a sickly hue besides. He shuddered.

Each of the *Eneph* mounted his beast and sat bare-back upon it, his torch raised.

"Now we will ride even like the East Wind," the Seer intoned, holding up and spreading wide his great arms, "and spread Hell-Fire wherever we tread."

The *Eneph* gave a cry that shook the air around them and to Lamech it was like an assault upon his very person. He staggered on his feet. At once, the giant, winged horses sprang away, their riders baying and holding aloft their torches.

The sound of the beasts' hooves shook the earth beneath him as they powered their way over the grassy hill directly before them and toward the Town beyond.

There would be no warning for Aheh-Raspuh, the Town that lay in their path.

He had condemned it by his very actions - their lord.

Lamech let out a low growl from deep in his throat.

Dalkus's special assassins had effectively dispatched all of Hen-Kiduh's guards as well, hadn't he? A lovely business that had been. That fool, even now, was probably resting in blissful ignorance on his perfumed bed.

Yes, and perhaps with one of his slave-girls. Or slave-boys.

Or maybe both with a goat thrown in as well. It made no difference now.

Lamech smiled.

"Dalkus!" he barked. He thrust out his hand toward the slowly receding din of the thundering *Eneph*.

He saw Dalkus raise his sword and then the infantry, hidden within a defile of the rise, began to move out. He signalled his charioteer and the man brought the war-machine alongside him. He took his helm and donned it.

Next to him, the Seer stirred. "I will climb the rise," he boomed out, "and raise the All-Father above the Town until it dies beneath his gaze!" The King could see him fingering the great, black talisman of the Serpent that hung by a chain around his throat.

Lamech nodded and stepped into his chariot. He gripped the charioteer's shoulder and the vehicle jolted off after the Army.

Ah! Let the sweet, red flow begin!

The Town of Aheh-Raspuh was situated in a depression in the grasses of the Plain; almost in a bowl. Lamech saw this now very clearly from the slightly higher vantage point of his chariot as he bore down upon it in the wake of his Army. He could see the *Eneph* dispersing, far ahead, quickly enveloping the pathetic, wooden walls of the city, hemming it in on all sides, the hooves of their infernal mounts kicking up blinding sheets of flame with their impossible speed! *Any faster and the damned things would fly!* He saw them spread the fire of their torches all through the grass surrounding the Town.

The wind, fierce now against his face as he went with his own speed in his chariot, was whipping and stoking the fires into a giant conflagration and blowing the flames swiftly toward the Town. Even as he watched its paltry walls alit in a horrifying inferno.

Soon there came to his ears the old familiar cries and screams.

Terror. He swallowed again and brought his bronze blade out of its sheath. He felt his sword-hand tremble with the familiar anticipation.

Blood. Death. They see it! They feel it!

And so do I!

The next few, swift hours were a red haze.

They brought Hen-Kiduh, bloodied and bound in chains, to the foot of a high, makeshift platform just before midday. Lamech looked down upon him from atop the wooden plinth. The Seer stood beside him, his great eyes closed as if in meditation. The air was still full of the smoke of the fires and the sun was dim in a grey sky above the dead city.

The king sat upon a bench made of planks of sturdy Oak, that wood which the Seer had proclaimed most sacred to the All-Father, and which alone had survived the burning in salvageable pieces. A pelt of aurochs hide had been thrown over it. In his lap, his great-sword lay, its blade naked.

Lamech signalled with a bronze-gauntleted hand and the two soldiers who had brought the prisoner at once grasped him by his tattered, bloodied robes and dragged him up the steps to the platform, hurling him at the King's very feet.

"Traitor," said the King.

"My liege!" the broken man gasped in a hoarse voice, looking up. His chains clinked together. "I swear to you on my life! Never did I do treason! I am loyal! I am true!"

"Another word and your tongue will be ripped out!" snapped Lamech. "I know that you sent messages to Lorban, to Suzzidz, maybe even to Lod. Did you think to hit me while I was dedicating at the Tower to the All-Father? You're probably in league with the Sethite."

Hen-Kiduh went pale as a white cloud, his lacerated face a ghastly pallor. "No!" he croaked. He made as if to jerk to his feet but his guards pummelled him down to the floor of the high dais again.

The King stared down at him with glowing eyes. "The other towns are already destroyed - as is now yours. Their Lords have been given over to the Great Father's Code and the All-Father's Wrath. But maybe….." He drew off the gauntlets from his hands and then lifted his right toward the prisoner. Its third finger bore the Signet Ring. "…..you wish to kiss the Royal Emblem and beg the King's mercy?"

Hen-Kiduh gaped up at him for a moment. "Y-yes! I will kiss the Emblem! I will beg the King!"

With scrabbling hands, he reached for Lamech's but, grimacing, the King snatched it back. "No, Fool!" he screamed. "Wretch!" He pointed a shaking finger at the Seer. "Let me first see you kiss the Image and beg *HIM* for mercy! Then perhaps I will!"

The Seer stirred and his huge, red eyes opened and smouldered down upon Hen-Kiduh.

The prisoner's jaw fell slack and his eyes became glassy with terror.

The Seer opened the folds of his great, robed *shendyt* and withdrew the dark talisman of the All-Father. He held it out before the fallen man and its ruby eyes seemed to smoulder.

Only garbled and strangled sounds emanated from Hen-Kiduh's throat.

After two heart-beats, the Seer rumbled, "The All-Father does not count him worthy to kiss his Image."

Lamech's dark lips twisted into a leer. "No, I think not," he purred. Then…..

"Bare his right arm!" he screamed.

The two soldiers again seized Hen-Kiduh and one thrust up the tatters of his robe to his right shoulder.

It was there, for all to see, scarred and bored into the Traitor's skin, above the elbow. Lamech's eyes fastened upon it.

"The Mark," he whispered. "The Hook and the Stick. The Sign of the Great Father." He licked his dark lips and then darted his eyes to the face of the Lord of lost Aheh-Raspuh. "You are not worthy to bear it."

In an instant, the King was on his feet, his great-sword clutched in both hands and then the blade was slicing downward in a great, vicious arc.

The arm of the prisoner was hewn from his body.

"Bring him!" screamed Lamech, then, and once more the soldiers took hold of Hen-Kiduh, now in shock and with a welter of blood spilling from his broken body.

They dragged him, swooning on his feet, his face as white as a bright cloud, bloodless, to the very edge of the high platform, next to the King and the Seer.

Before them was a forest of up-thrusted spears, their butts rammed into the soft, torn ground near the ruined city and their sharp tips pointing up toward the dulled sky. Lamech motioned with his arm to them and several nearby already bore the broken and bloodied bodies of several women, still clad in shredded robes and finery.

"Your wife and daughters were handed over to the tender mercies of the soldiers before I showed *them* mercy!" screamed the King at the prisoner, only now the man was barely conscious. He had to be held up by his escort, for his legs could not bear him. "And your sons…..well, they are even now being flayed by my great Allies." His eyes flicked to the looming figure beside them before gleaming once more upon the ghost of a man swaying before him. "They have a particular…..taste….. for sacrificing Traitors alive in the pits of their Mountains, I am told. If your sons survive the journey, that is….."

Then, seeing that it was over, he nodded to the soldiers and they threw down Hen-Kiduh upon the spear-tips, his lifeless body joining those of his family in death.

"They bear your Seed, you see," murmured Lamech, looking down upon his work, seeing that it was well done, "and all Traitors' Seed belongs to the Serpent."

A knock sounded upon the Chamber door.

The Queen tensed, sitting before her bronze mirror. There had been no word from the King and her own plans were not yet ripe. She had ordered quiet and privacy so that she might make them so but bored and sullen, having failed to find the single spark, the catalyst that would bring them to life, had commanded the slaves to tend to her instead. One was, even now, paring and buffing the nails of her left hand with a small, coarse hand-stone while the other stood behind, gathering her long, ebon hair into elaborate braids, entwining it with a thin, golden chain.

At the knock, she shot her right hand into the air and the two slave-girls froze where they stood. Turning her head, carefully, so that her hair did not leave the slave's grasp, she hissed, "Li-et!"

At once, the small shadow detached itself from the far corner of her gilt-framed, grand bed. It moved beyond the flicker of the taper set within the bronze sconce on the wall above the table where she sat. She watched as it slipped, noiselessly, to the huge door of the room and held up two small, trembling hands before its sturdy Oaken frame.

Adah could hear a soft, intake of breath.

"It is Ohun," whispered the child at the door. There was another pause and another ghostly breath. "The scent of the High Plain is upon him….."

"Let him come!" said the Queen, suddenly, and immediately the small slave-girl reached for the latch of the huge door and lifted it.

The Chamberlain of the Palace stood in the open doorway.

"My Queen, I bear a message from the King!" he announced, "He desires to inform Their Majesties, The Queens of the World, that he and his great Allies have been victorious over the foul and base Traitors of the High Plain! He enjoins them to pay all due honour to the Great Father and all due subjection to the All-Father! He returns to the Great City with all haste."

"I hear, Ohun!" answered the Queen after a suitable moment from her table and in a loud voice, "Fealty and Devotion to the King! All Honour and Subjection to the Great Father and to the All-Father!"

Ohun bowed deeply. "May it be so!" he effused in his deep voice.

And then it came to her in a flash; that which she had long sought. The way forward - the catalyst!

When he comes, the Blood-Lust will yet be upon him. Do I not know it well? He will want his wine. And then he will want.….. She trembled with excitement. *Now you shall receive your due, Woman!*

Adah licked her lips. "Ohun!" she cried. The Chamberlain stood rigid within the doorway. "This is most excellent news! You will go at once to the kitchens and inform them that I will host the King and his officers at Table this evening. There shall be a banquet; a great feast! Meat and wine and dancing, as it pleases the King. Now, go to Adjeek and have him choose six of the King's most-favourite slave-girls of the North - those whose skin is as white as goat's milk and who are most versed in the dancing arts - and prepare them for the most splendid occasion! And then - " She paused. Ohun stood where he was, not a tremble visible in his frame. Seeing this, satisfied that not a word was missing him, she continued, " - and then you will go to the apartments of Her Majesty, Queen Zillah of the North, and invite her to sit with me as my honoured guest at Table. She shall sit upon my right hand and the King shall sit upon my left."

The Chamberlain blinked but made no other movement or sound.

"Do you understand these instructions, Ohun?"

"I do, My Queen, and - " He darted his eyes to her " - if I may, I hasten to obey them with gladness of heart."

Then he was turning and rushing from the open doorway.

Li-et silently closed the huge Oak door after him.

"Resume," growled Adah, eyeing the slave-girls in the polished bronze balefully. "I must look beautiful for the King tonight." At once, they continued with their tasks. *But not the most beautiful.* She smiled, a slow curl of a lip at one end in the shining bronze. She raised her right hand again. "My pet," she murmured.

The small girl with the milky eyes came out of the shadows and glided to the Queen's side.

The other slaves attending her trembled but carried on without pause.

Adah leant forward slightly, carefully, over her desk, trying not to tug her hair. She reached across her table and retrieved an ivory box. This she slid to the corner of the table-top, nearest the blind waif, and opened it, turning it toward the girl.

"Touch, My Love," the Queen said softly, *"See."*

The child reached into the box and withdrew a shining ring. She brought it to her mouth and bit its edge with tiny, razor-like teeth. "Gold," Li-et whispered.

"A gift with which I had thought to honour the King, in anticipation of his great victory," said the Queen, "but which now I will offer to *her* with my compliments instead." Li-et returned the ring to the box but as her tiny hand again lay within it, it froze.

"Ah, My Pet," murmured the Queen, seeing the slender, supple hand tremble within the box, "I have added something special to make it just right. The perfect token with which to honour her." She darted her eyes to the blind child's face. "You see why I entrust it only to you, My Love, and to no-one else. At the proper time, you will give it to her."

The thin arm withdrew once more and went very slowly to the waif's side. "My Mistress will say the word," Li-et whispered, "and I will give it."

Ohun was returning from the kitchens in the belly of the Palace where he had issued the Queen's instructions and had finished mounting the hidden steps when the noise reached his sharp, always alert ears. He turned into the corridor that would take him to Adjeek and the *hareem,* when suddenly from behind, from the direction of the smaller, Western doors of the Palace, there surged toward him two, huge black shapes followed by a scrambling third.

He had seen enough of *them* recently to know exactly who the shapes were.

Eneph! Have we not had our bellies full of them?

Halting, he drew himself up and forced himself to confront them as they came forward swiftly along the opulent passage, trampling the luxurious carpets under their feet, their gigantic, booming foot-falls shaking the walls. The third figure, a Guard, hastened near and stood behind and apart from them.

The *Eneph,* seeing Ohun, stopped two great strides from him. Ohun was suddenly startled to see that they gripped another, smaller figure between them in their massive hands.

A man.

But who? The poor wretch's head was covered in a hood that looked to have been rammed over his head and his wrists were roughly bound with one of their frightening hair ropes. He did not utter a sound.

"We need to see your *king!*" spat the one *Eneph.* "Now!" He had glowing blue eyes, this one. They beat upon Ohun like hammers.

"We've caught one of them that he'll like to see, Servant," rumbled the second and this one's huge, lamp-like eyes were a deep, emerald green.

"I'm sorry, Master Chamberlain," panted the Guard, then, still behind the giants. Indeed, there was no room in the corridor for him to step past them. "As there is no clear compact with our Allies, I did not hinder them."

"As if you could!" snapped the first *Eneph,* impatiently, not turning to face him, but keeping his liquid glare upon Ohun.

Ohun raised his hand toward the two guests. *I must treat them in the one manner that they do not expect.*

"I am afraid the King is away on campaign with your….. Seer," he said, briskly. "You will have to either await his return while housed in a Guest Room or give full custody of this man to me until he returns. I am the highest ranking officer of the Palace currently within its walls."

There was a heavy silence. Speechless, the two *Eneph* looked at one another.

"He is ours….." began the first in a terrible growl, eyes a-smoulder, but suddenly the second thrust up his hand before his companion.

"He is a Sethite," boomed the green-eyed *Eneph* at Ohun, "and you are a Cainite. What matters these things to us? My brother and I do not care about the petty, lowly, grievances of your 'Great Fathers.' We will give him to you." The other went rigid for a moment and turned quickly toward him but Ohun saw that the second's hand remained firmly at the other's huge chest. "BUT," went on the second giant, in a low, dangerous voice that made even Ohun swallow, "when he leads your King to other, better Sethites, we will go with him and what we take then will be ours indeed. And you shall not have it."

A shiver stole through Ohun but he raised his voice and bellowed into the hall: "So shall it be! Before the Great Father Cain and the All-Father who dwells within the Mountains, I agree to these terms. Now…..release and reveal your prisoner."

The second *Eneph* snatched the hood from the hidden man's head.

The prisoner raised his eyes and looked at Ohun and they were sharp and black, as was his weathered, lined face. He wiped his mouth with the back of his hand. "I am a Sethite, yes," he said, quietly, "And it's True, I do serve Noah, the Master of the Valley of Seth. But I have a different 'Father' than you do. He is the One, True God. *Abba Father* is His name." The black eyes did not blink. "And mine is A-Phthah."

X

The Stranger's voice came out of the swirling mists and it was all around him. He could not escape it. *Only He is not the Stranger anymore! He revealed Himself to me! He is the Friend; He is MY Friend!*

But he shuddered, there in the twisting, roiling mists as he listened to that voice, and heard those words:

"I will put an end to all people."

An end. The End is the Beginning!

The fire had long gone, the flames of the bonfire extinguished. He was not there anymore, amongst the foothills. Now there was only the wind.

THE WIND!

He was falling through the mist, arms and legs flailing helplessly, and the wind was slapping his face with ice-cold hands from the high Mountains in the West. A darkness, terrible and deep, was swelling there, reaching out toward him.

He turned to look at it in terror and the words came again:

"For the Earth is filled with violence because of them."

The voice seemed to pulse through every fibre of his being:

"I will surely destroy both them and the Earth."

Everything and everyone!

There were flashes of light all around him now. They split the darkness with jagged bolts but he could see nothing else. Far, far below he saw the black ground. Only it was not the ground any longer for it seemed to ebb and flow, swell and recede in moving ridges and valleys!

"Everything on the Earth will perish," said the voice, "All life under the heavens will cease. Every creature that has the breath of life in it - "

He tried to scream but nothing came out.

" - for I will bring the Flood."

He cried out and felt his body jerk. His heart was racing and sweat stood out on his forehead and slicked his tired, worn body.

He lay upon a low pallet, covered in furs and underneath a gently swelling and moving hide ceiling. Everything was still a chaos in his mind; swirling, nebulous shapes. Except words burst through the fog inside his head, as strong as thunder and as clear as sunlight:

Therefore, go and build yourself an -

He sat bolt-upright.

A tiger was peering at him through huge, golden eyes no more than five forearms away.

"Teegerees," he murmured, stunned.

An ostrich loomed behind it, its head brushing the hide ceiling of the tent.

Now he could only stare.

"Master!" cried a high voice, then.

A boy ran forward, swallowing, and halted between tiger and ostrich. Noah, watching, could see his wide eyes swivelling from one to the other. "I was to keep watch at your door but….. the Animals are becoming too many! They are Tame! They are finding all manner of new caves along the River, even up to the Mountains and they are coming more and more every day *from* the Mountains and from far down the Valley too!" He heaved a great breath into his small chest. "I do not know why. The Masters Shem and Japheth do not know why. I cannot stop them! No-one can! Forgive me! I - I was to let the Masters know when you…..awoke."

The old man continued to stare, dumbly, moving his eyes from animal to animal and then to boy. A heavy silence followed and then the young lad burst out again, "I helped you at the falling waters, Master!"

"I must see it," croaked Noah, heedless, suddenly. One thought had penetrated the shadows, the unsettling Dream, and it was now his one and only ray of light; his all-consuming hope. The echoes of the Friend's - of *Abba Father's* - words still filled his head. Struggling free of the hide covers of his bed, he got to his feet, swaying perilously.

"Where is my staff?" he grated.

The boy, thinking at first to help steady his Master, jerked back and then ran to fetch the old man's staff instead. "Show it to me!" barked Noah again, snatching the long stick from him with whitened, clutching fingers.

Time was of the essence. "In the Name of *Abba Father,* show me what has been done so far! For I know it has already begun."

Upon the Eastern side of the fording place, across from the bustle of the field where the men laboured at their great task, Japheth stood in the far, ancient Barley field facing back toward the beginning of the High Valley. He was both perplexed and astonished.

"And when did you first notice this?" he asked the pasture-lad.

The boy threw up his thin arms, as if in utter helplessness. "Which one, Master? The Grains or the Shrubs or the Birds - "

Japheth sliced a hand in the air, not wholly in irritation but with a touch of bemusement. He recognized the lad as one of those who had been with Father at the great water-fall. "I know about the Grains," he said, briskly, "a Miracle from *Abba Father* without a 'grain' of doubt" - he smiled to himself at his own wit - "preserved intact in one of these innumerable Caves next the River. And the Birds, well - " He glanced up at the sky uneasily where several, high, dark circling forms continued to fly above them against the dimming, bronze canopy, crying ceaselessly.

In the Western expanse of that same sky, up there, even now, he knew, the black hands were slowly reaching across the Earth. He shivered. It's what he and his brother had begun calling them. He saw the hint of them in the corner of his eye even now but did not look directly at them. He had seen enough of them. Doggedly, he said to the lad, "No, it's the shrubs I want to hear about. That's the real reason I came to talk to you. It sounded strange."

The boy's eyes went wide and he nodded vigorously. "The shrubs," he said, pointing past Japheth. "Yes! They grow out from the River toward the distant Mountains in the North in a narrowing finger for a length of a hundred forearms and then stop."

"I know," said Japheth, growing impatient, "What don't I know?"

"They separate the one lost, old grain field from the other like an arm!"

"Millet to the West, Barley to the East," Japheth put in, sighing.

"Even so," said the boy, still eager and wide-eyed and nodding all at once, "and the Animals will not pass from one to the other in front of its tip! They go back and squeeze through beside the River and the bushes and then go around to the other field from there instead!"

"What do you mean they won't - ?" Japheth broke off and looked up.

Even at that moment, there were four mules near to the shrubs' tip, upon their side, nosing at the ancient stubble of Barley. He watched them for a moment. There *was* something odd that he had noticed about the movement of the pack animals that were left here at the grain fields to graze - when they had to be rested from the great work going on across the Fording Place. Something.

And it is Abba Father's Master Plan rather than Father's, as it turns out, that we are all labouring at over there isn't it? Could….. ABBA FATHER HIMSELF have changed the beasts somehow as they work on that extraordinary Thing over there? He furrowed his brows, looking at the out-thrusted finger of the bushes. *Like a Verge they are too, as if bordering a dwelling or encircling something; protecting it.*

But whose dwelling? What are they protecting?

Suddenly, his own master plan occurred to him.

Without warning, he bolted toward the mules, shouting and waving his hands.

The beasts broke off their grazing and shot up their heads to look at him, ears pricked and standing straight up like shoots. After a moment, and seeing that he showed no sign of slowing down or ceasing his odd behaviour, they reluctantly turned away, stumbling at first and then trotting off toward the South, wickering and murmuring as they went. One, however, being more to his right, at first veered North. Almost immediately, however, giving a spastic jerk of its body, it twisted around and, showing the whites of its eyes, galloped after the others away to the South, giving out a strange crying sound.

"I'll be hided!" Japheth burst out, panting, watching them go. He shook his head. "What does it mean?"

The boy came running up beside him. "I told you, Master!" he gasped. "I told you!"

"Yes," said Japtheth, letting out a breath. "You certainly did. And now I've seen the phenomenon myself. But I'll be plucked and shucked if I know what it tells us!" He fixed the lad with an intense stare. "What say we go and see what we can see?" And immediately, he began walking where the one Animal would not.

Gasping, the boy balked and would not follow.

Japheth headed straight for the end of the bushes, striding over the dry stubble of the Barley field. Distantly, he was aware of his heart knocking against his ribs and a latent fear in the back of his mind. He laughed to himself. *Nonsense! What is there to fear?*

He stood at the Verge's very tip.

He waited, heart throbbing.

Nothing happened.

Slowly, he turned to look back at the boy, still standing far off in the Barley stubble, open-mouthed. "You know," he called out to him, as casually as he could, and gesturing with his hand at the bushes, "the Ancient told me once that Beasts can sense things that Men cannot. And I have come to believe it. There could have been an Earth-Shake here a thousand Season-Turns ago. Hmm? Or even a Land-Slide. Who knows? It could even have affected the very ground around here. Or the crops. Or maybe even - " He broke off again as a new thought struck him. "Maybe something is *hiding* in here….."

Trembling all over, he leant into the bushes and reached forward with his arms, pushing aside their scraggly, dark green and grey limbs. He gasped.

"Ah! Father!"

Shem was striding toward him, kicking through the long grass that covered the field where the men worked.

"You looked dead tired after you bellowed out all of those astounding instructions at us two days ago," said the young Master with a thin smile. "Japheth is yonder there - " He jerked his head toward the East, "investigating mysterious bushes. I think. Sometimes I have no idea *what* he is doing. Yesterday, he was scouting out where the Animals are sheltering. Many more have come since you retired to your tent. Some very big. Some very small. All quiet. And that *wind* that you warned us about….. My Cloak and Staff and Sandals! If you hadn't done so we'd all be flat smudges in the Valley by now!" He turned and gave a grand sweep of his hand toward the West, where now there was only a great open space clear to the distant foothills, with nary a tree to bar the view. "It took down everything as neat as you please. All of that big, old, scary Forest. And now we have all of the wood that we can handle for your ingenious….. Plan!"

He nodded vigorously. "We've got all the servants hauling and splitting the logs, of course, laying out the beams and planks. And then some are also hammering and nailing the sides with thin spikes." He paused, looking intently at his father. "It was amazing," he said in a lower voice. "We found them in the caves along the River where we had sheltered from the wind. Just what we needed when we needed it! To do this - your….. Ark. Just like *Abba Father* said." He nodded down at his feet, where a giant picture had been scored, scuffed, pulled out of the very grass. It was a vast shape, a shape of something that had never before been seen upon the Earth - and perhaps would never be seen again.

The shape from his dreams.

Noah, hearing and looking at all of this, but not listening or seeing, then gazed past his son to the field.

Toiling beasts. Groaning men. All were there, working, labouring.

And in their midst -

The Ark.

So it is not only a dream after all - it is REAL!

There, indeed, in that cleared field, before him, the behemoth of wood was taking shape - three hundreds of forearms long and fifty wide! When it was done, he knew it would be thirty high as well, for the words of *Abba Father* still shook him in his sandals.

It is the only way, He said. The only way to go through - to go through….. *what is to come.*

The End.

Yet not the End!

Only the keel was laid and the lower deck of the Ark completed as yet. The middle and upper decks were still to be done before…..

"Time," he burst out, suddenly.

"Pardon?" said Shem, giving a start.

Noah turned to look at him and his eyes bore into his son's. "You said 'two days ago' that I bellowed these instructions, yes?"

Shem nodded.

"What else did I say?"

Shem turned his eyes away and watched the men working on the Ark for a moment. Noah suddenly noticed the Animals looking on, watching. Two Zebras idly cropped the long grass of the field toward the Southern foothills, not thirty strides from the nearest man, and yet there could be no doubt that they were…..watching. And over to the West there stood a pair of Giraffes, gazing solemnly at the labourers!

They are waiting for the Thing to be done. Waiting for the End to come, for the -

Involuntarily, Noah slid his eyes to the sky and sensed his son doing the same.

It was near to midday, for the sun was high - and yet, its light was eerily dimmed and the sky was like bronze. Had he grown used to this unreal sky that was not bright and this sun that did not shine properly already? The vapours, the streaming fingers from out of the West, were now almost half-way across the huge, bronze dome of the heavens. And they were darkening and thickening, undulating like enormous snakes. He watched their scary limbs slowly reaching across the sky. There was still a wind in the West, from the gap between the great arms of the Mountains to both North and South and now that the Forest was no longer here to shield it, it was bringing a cold that seemed to make the growing darkness that much more unbearable.

Oh, Abba Father, I believe in the words you have spoken. I believe in YOU! Help my unbelief!

Noah jerked his head toward Shem. "What other 'instructions' did I give you?" He was all but shouting now. "Before I went insensible! What else did I *say?*"

The young Master - his son - looked back at him, blankly, for a moment. "You told them to take two other men with them," he swallowed, "because that was all that could be spared. To take them and go as quickly as possible to fetch the rest of the Family back from the Valley of Seth. To bring them here as fast as possible."

Noah shivered and closed his eyes. "And who did I say this to?"

"To Artuah, the Archer, and to your old servant. A-Phthah. They left two days ago."

XI

Above him, distantly, he could hear the clamour of the music. It had been going on for some time now. The beat of the drummers could be felt even within the damp, cold, stone walls behind him. He turned and lifted his hands, in their heavy, bronze shackles and touched the wet rock wall of his cell. He was well beneath the Palace here, he knew. A distant throbbing moved within the wall. He turned his head and looked behind him, over his shoulder, into the gloom. Beyond the metal bars of his cage, only the faintest hint of a corridor could be made out - the one long passageway of the dungeon that he had traversed, staggering, what seemed an Age ago already. There was a torch in a sconce somewhere back there along that stone corridor and its feeble light just reached him where he stood.

And now the great Fool feasts and drinks up above while his world is about to face Abba Father's righteous Judgement!

Or am I the fool too? How could I have let myself be taken? And so easily? It matters not who did it, for am I afraid of them?

He scoffed into the gloom.

He had gone ahead. After the Water-Fall, he had allowed himself to become separated from Artuah and the scouts. *Too eager! Too ready to please the Master, I was! Abandoning reason and rushing headlong into their dug pit like a -*

A fool, yes.

Sighing, he took his hands from the wall and sat down heavily on the cold, hard-packed, dirt floor, his back propped up against the equally cold stone.

"But Artuah has reached the rest of the Family by now," he murmured roughly in the dimness. "The Mistress and the Young Master and all of the Good-Daughters. They are moving toward the Master's and *Abba Father's*

Safe Place even now." But the sound of his own voice uttering these words in that dread darkness did not reassure him of their Truth. He shivered and tried to relax, to calm his thoughts.

He had folded his arms across his chest and had half-closed his eyes when suddenly the tiny hairs all over his body sprang upright. He gave a jerk.

Merciful Father, something is near!

He became rigid, staring, straining his eyes into the darkness. "Who's there?" he croaked and his voice was hoarse with disuse.

A shadow stood at the bars of his cell.

"They revel now," it whispered, "My Mistress and the King and the Other One. Yet the time draws short."

A-Phthah sat upon the dirt floor, heart thudding. *What is this?* "Who - ?" he started to say but stopped. He caught a glimpse of small hands curled around metal bars, of a tiny head, as black and as featureless as an abyss, stuck in between them.

A child? He shivered again. *A shadow.*

"They will come for you soon," the shadow-child hissed, "and then you will know it."

A fiend of the Enemy! He began to breathe more rapidly, the air moving almost fluidly in and out of his lungs. Shuddering, he murmured, "Know what?"

"Pain," came the whisper across the dirt floor.

A bolt of fear stabbed through him. *Ah, Abba Father, am I to be tested then? Is that why I have failed You - failed My Master - to learn what True Obedience means?*

He could make out the small head cocking at him through the bars. A soft sighing breath came to his straining ears. "You are of the Valley of Seth," the shadow whispered again, "The one that defies the King. I can smell it on you."

"I defy your King, yes!" he blurted out in a ghastly voice into the gloom that pressed in on him now, sucking the warmth and the life right out of him. He gasped for breath. "I defy him! I do not fear him! And neither does My Master!"

"You have Power," the shadow-child murmured, hoarsely. "It too I can feel on you. You do not fear for your own life. It is for this reason that I have come. My Mistress desires it."

"You do not serve your King, then?" he asked, roughly, sardonically.

"I serve only My Mistress and *she* has pledged herself and her soul only to the real king - my king. The All-Father!"

BLASPHEMY! Abba Father, save me!

Shuddering all over, he grated, "There is a greater King than yours, Witch-ling, and His name is *Abba Father!*"

Another hiss came from the shadow-child as he spoke that Name and he saw the tiny fingers twist around the metal bars like snakes and then shake them so violently that they groaned perilously in their bronze foundations bolted to the stone floor!

He felt his jaw slacken as he gaped at her, heart hammering in his temples.

Truly this World must End! Truly it must be Renewed! It is a Demon with which I speak!

He began, at once, to Pray and immediately the small hands released the cell bars and vanished into the darkness.

"What's all this?" thundered a harsh voice, and a flicker of orange light cleaved the shadows around him.

Swooning, he looked up into the cold, cruel features of his jailer and they seemed to twist and writhe in the flickering light of his torch. The man stood in the open doorway of his cell, the torch in one hand and a whip of leather thongs in the other. Two more men, big and burly with leering faces stood on either side of him. "Loose him and get him on his feet," growled the jailer to them, but his eyes were on the prisoner. "We'll teach these Southern Sethite slaves how we do things here on the Plain." As the other two men came forward, he spat a dark, thick gob of foulness at A-Phthah's feet. The prisoner sat, heaving, still spent from his encounter with the shadow-waif, upon the dirt floor. "That's for your precious Valley," scorned the jailer, "and for your 'Great Father.'"

It was a crude instrument, he saw at once. Rough hewn, wooden planks filled with splinters and knots, hammered together - a straight, narrow, horizontal beam supported by a perpendicular trestle at both ends.

He saw at once that at each end, the infernal contraption bore a length of bronze chain coiled around a huge drum with a metal crank. At the end of each chain lay a pair of bronze shackles. All of the metal was so tarnished that it appeared to be one and the same colour as the omnipresent, hard-packed, earthen floor.

He swallowed hard in his dry, sharp throat.

Two more guards came and lit the four torches smeared in tallow that stood in the bronze stanchions at the four corners of the small, dank room.

Then he was grabbed by his two escorts and his first instinct was to flail his arms wildly at them, writhe his body, wrench it from their grasp, do anything to keep them from moving him closer to that thing! But the head jailer was there next to him in an instant, his fetid breath causing A-Phthah's nostrils to flare.

"It is better for you if you don't resist," the jailer grunted in his ear, "but better for me if you do." He then punched A-Phthah sharply in the ribs and the older man doubled up in pain, coughing and spluttering. "Get him on the Table!" snarled the jailer and the two men all but lifted him off of the ground and slammed him hard onto the wooden contraption. Dimly, he heard it groaning beneath his weight. At once, the other two guards came forward and, together, the four of them began stretching out his body and placing the bronze shackles upon his wrists and ankles. The jailer watched with glittering, black eyes. He began to gasp and groan as they next turned the cranks on the two drums. Soon his arms and legs were drawn taut by the chains and he gave out a sharp cry.

The jailer shot his hand into the air and the cranks ceased. He came and stood at the side of A-Phthah's head and his eyes were also like shadows.

"The Table is a splendid thing," the jailer crooned, softly. "It prepares the one who lies upon it so well that when the King comes he will sell his own mother to be free of it. He will sing like a bird." He leaned down farther until his nose was an inch from A-Phthah's. "And so you will."

Abba Father, my body is in Your hands!

The jailer raised his hand again.

And Pain made itself known in Truth.

Fire was burning somewhere. Smoke filled his nostrils. His head spun wildly.

Beneath him the floor was rolling!

Back and forth it tossed him, up and down, until he felt quite ill.

"Stop," he murmured from a burning throat, "Please. STOP!"

He could remember the pain, every inch of his body afire. How long had it been his constant companion now? The taste of blood was in his mouth. Oh, it had been darkness and agony for ages without end! Surely, Truly, it was so! Why did the floor not just open up and swallow him whole and he would be free of it at last?

He was struck full in the face.

"Wake up, Sethite! You have a guest."

His eyes fluttered open. *I am not dead.* He could see nothing. His eyes felt red and swollen. Then, above him, a damp stone ceiling swam slowly into view.

He sensed the jailer standing nearby again, his hand raised and his fist clenched.

A voice, sharp and cold and venomous, snapped, "Leave us!"

The hand quickly lowered and the dim form of the jailer slunk away, bowing. In its place, wrapped in black shadow, stood another.

"I am Adah," it said to him quietly, "the Queen of the World."

He licked his parched lips. "No," he whispered, using what strength was left to him, "The Queen of the Damned."

A sharp pain lanced through his side. He cried out, shuddering, upon the wooden beam, arms and legs rigid. "Is that how you speak to My Mistress?" hissed a voice, one he knew well for it haunted all of his dreams now and drove his pain; fed on it. It was as if it came from the very air around him.

The Queen raised her hand. "My Pet," she murmured and at once the pain subsided and he gasped again, trying to take in as much blessed oxygen into his lungs as he could. Hoarse coughs wracked his spent body.

Adah lowered her face to his and he could see the sharp blue of her eyes in the torchlight and through the haze of the smoke that made his head reel. He saw her ruby-red lips hover above him and he watched them with riveted eyes as they moved again. "You will give me something before the King comes," they whispered, "and perhaps I will give you something in return."

At this, she lifted her hand again and behold! this time there was a dagger in it! He stared at it through swollen eyes. Its hilt in her hand was as black as the shadows that surrounded them but its thin blade shone in the flames of the torches with a pale light. She lowered its tip and laid it gently against his left cheek. Then she pressed it so that it pierced his skin.

He gave out a garbled, broken cry.

"Release," she breathed, her dark, blue eyes boring into his and his own were drawn to them like moths to a flame. He could not resist them. "No more Pain. No more suffering. Ah! Only…..give me the secret," she hissed. "The secret of your God. How can I gain his Power?"

He tried to shake his head but that blade stood cold against his flesh. "Can't…..gain….. His power," he grated, "only…..stand True….within it."

The tip of the blade withdrew from his cheek but then he felt its cruel metal touching his cracked lips. He shivered. "I can offer you other things," she whispered, and, taking away the angry knife, she brought her own, red lips near instead, lightly brushing them against his. "Pleasure," she whispered. And now he was ashamed for he felt the cold of the metal disappear from his spent body and be replaced by a stoking heat.

Abba Father I am weak! Keep me True to You - True to the Master! Keep me thus in the face of this vile schemer!

There came a dull, distant clank of metal in the far reaches of the dungeon.

It seemed to reverberate within the damp walls and the Queen withdrew from him a span. He sensed her rigidity.

"Mistress," came the whisper in the air, "it is the King. He comes for his prize."

"No," growled the Queen and he saw her shadow-eyes gaze down at him and this time it was they that gleamed with a pale light.

Then the dagger was raised once more high above his chest!

It was a moment, an eternity. He saw the blade bury itself deep in his chest, saw his life begin to rise up from his body as if they were joined only by a single thread, so fine, so slender. And the thought gladdened his aching heart! *Abba Father, receive me! I am Yours.*

But he was not slain.

At least not yet.

Nevertheless, in the bitter end, he did fall. For the King did come, with his great-sword, screaming that there was no time, that Darkness was covering all the world. His abdomen was laid bare by the mighty sword's edge and his entrails threatened to be pulled from his body by the King's own, bloody hands!

And so he had sung like that bird! To his shame.

The Water-Fall, the hidden passage, the Valley of Stone, the location of the Master and of all of the Family of Seth! Even, as far as he understood it, *Abba Father's* great Plan itself.

Everything was given over to the Lord of Cain.

And then at long last he knew no more.

XII

"Too much time has been lost!" Lamech spat. "While my Enemy gloats at me for having lost him!"

He stood in the Main Chamber with the Heavenly Lights arrayed above them, looking down upon them all assembled there with infinite indifference. His aides, pale and terrified, struggled and fumbled with his breast-plate. Ramming his hands into his leather and bronze-plated gauntlets, he whirled and thundered, "Bring him!"

They brought him. He was only a ghost of a man now. His face was waxy and his eyes were sunken into his skull, no more than tiny black holes lost within a thin, bony face. His black hair was tangled and chunks of it had been ripped from his bleeding scalp. He staggered between two soldiers but his leg-irons had been removed to allow him to walk. His wrists were securely shackled.

The King surveyed him with baleful eyes. "The Champion of Seth," he rumbled. "Noah's Pride and Prize."

The prisoner jerked and stared.

"Oh, yes," Lamech taunted and he laughed scornfully, a sound that was ghastly and which echoed around the vast, marble hall, "I know of this.....new name of his - or whatever it is that he is calling himself. Does he fancy himself a King? Does he not fear the Power of the Son of Cain?"

The prisoner made a rasping sound in his dry throat.

Lamech bore his eyes upon the wasted man. "What?" he snapped. "Speak up, Sethite! I can't hear your pigeon-jabber!"

"Wrong," croaked A-Phthah, "You're wrong."

"Shut him up," said Lamech.

A soldier moved forward and struck the prisoner, back-handed across the mouth with his own gauntleted hand. Blood sprayed from A-Phthah's split lips and a tooth landed at the King's very feet upon the marble floor.

Barking out a laugh, Lamech stuck out a booted toe and flicked it away. "You amuse me, Sethite," he taunted, "but I don't need you to talk. Just to point the way."

Dalkus, his helm under his arm and a squad of his best shock-troops behind him, entered briskly into the Chamber and approached. "The Army is ready, My King," he said. "I am leaving a garrison of recruits within the City but all of the veteran corps are assembled."

Lamech's eyes flashed. "Very well," he growled, "very well indeed. The last day of our Enemy is here. The last day of his existence upon this - " He broke off for now Ohun had come into the Chamber and behind him came Adah and Zillah, wearing their royal finery, and with their Crowns upon their heads.

"Ah!" The King turned to them and his face alit with a cold, radiant light. "My Queens!" They came forward together, standing several feet apart. "Upon the departure of the King's Army, you will go up to the Altar upon the Ziggurat. There, at the very Apex of the World, you will give such gifts and make such offerings as are due to the All-Father in token of our Great Father Cain's final victory over his Enemy - his own Traitorous brother Seth!"

The Queens bowed low.

Turning, Lamech growled at the prisoner, "You will ride with me in my chariot, Sethite." He rammed his helm down upon his head.

They all turned toward the great Doors.

Several tall, dark forms stood within the entrance of the Main Chamber, casting tall, dark shadows across the marble floor and barring their way.

The King, with Dalkus and the prisoner and the soldiers, drew up short.

The Seer stood before the entrance in his full, white *shendyt* and a dozen, huge *Eneph* in their half-*shendyts*, stood arrayed behind him, each clutching his spear, vast and thick and tipped with bronze. Lamech looked up into his great ally's wide, dark, sharply-browed face but the *Eneph's* huge, liquid, red eyes were inscrutable, as always.

A stillness came into the huge room and it was a stillness different from that which usually surrounded Lamech's great Allies. He could sense it.

A heartbeat passed, then two.

"Let us ride now, Great Friend," the King ventured at last and there was a quaver in his voice that he did not like. "Let us, together, witness our final victory!"

The Seer continued to stare in silence, holding him in his red glare.

"The King," he said at last in his deep rumble, "rides to his Destiny; the Destiny of Cain. But he rides alone."

Lamech gasped. "What is the meaning of this?" he growled. "We have declared our common goal! I have made Pledge to the All-Father in the name of Cain!" He shot out his right arm before the looming *Eneph*. "I bear the Mark!"

The Seer slowly lowered his red eyes to the King's bare arm and held it for long seconds. "The Son of Cain does indeed bear the Mark," he rumbled at last. "Yet the Mark of Cain is not the mark of the All-Father. *HE* is our true King. And now he calls us Home to the Deepest Pit beneath the Mountains."

"Calls you!" Lamech burst out. "What is this?"

"The World is changing. Fire cannot undo Water."

Lamech stood dumb as did all who stood with him. Outside there came the faintest rumble of thunder.

Then two huge figures burst forth from the ranks of *Eneph*. "We fight with the Lord of Men!" cried one. "We pledge to him our spears!" They brought the butts of their great weapons down upon the marble of the Chamber and the sound of it was like that thunder in Lamech's ears only much closer.

The Seer whirled to face them and for a long moment regarded them with blazing eyes. "Dawlgla. Bhagra. You defy the Order," he rumbled in a terrible voice.

"Then our Blood," answered Dawlgla, slickly, "will be on our own heads." His swimming, green eyes shot to Lamech. "We did not draw the Blood of him to whom we were sent."

Lamech gave a start at this.

"But now we will," put in Bhagra with a growl. "And let all who stand in our way - be he Brethren or Man or Animal - Bleed like he will."

The Seer drew himself up to his fullest height and he towered even over them. "So be it," he pronounced. He raised a giant fist into the air and at once the other *Eneph* arrayed behind him began to slip out of the Chamber as quickly and as silently as they had entered it. The Seer left last of all without a backward glance.

Lamech turned to face the two *Eneph* who remained.

"You shall walk by my chariot," he told them.

Dawlgla and Bhagra hefted their gigantic spears and grinned. And the sight of it made Lamech's stomach turn.

XIII

He found himself once again upon the River path. This time he was walking almost at a march. Ahead, Artuah and the two men who had come with him were fanned out before them in an echelon formation, each watching in his direction the River or the Path or the trees of the Valley. Their arrows were nocked to their bows all the time now. Artuah had mentioned the ambush of A-Phthah on their way to the Homestead and Ham knew that they were near now to the very place where it had happened. He glanced beside him. Mother was walking as briskly as he had ever seen her, her hood of ochre drawn up once more over her head. *There's no choice anymore, is there? We go and go fast or we die. That's what Artuah said. That's what he said that FATHER had said!*

"They hadn't even left the Valley," Ham whispered, teeth clenched, "Those two *Eneph.* They remained within the Valley of Seth and went and hid themselves somewhere and waited! Waited for an opportunity to show itself. And it did!"

Mother glanced at him for a moment as they went but then went back to looking out over the River. He saw her lips moving within the folds of her covering.

She Prays. She Prays for Father and my brothers and our wives.

He turned and looked behind him, trying to keep up the brisk pace along the winding Path as he did so. His two Good-Sisters came behind, their ochre scarves around their necks, with the Ancient, clutching his javelin, walking beside them. The few pack animals that they needed to bear their clothing and food were immediately behind them along with a handful of Household servants. Neltamuk, his Beloved and his Betrothed, however, was not with her sisters for she had insisted on accompanying her parents at the very back. They and the rest of the servants from

94

the South - all those who were Bonded to Seth - had insisted upon accompanying the rest of the Family out of the Valley. And this even though none of them would -

Oh, Abba Father!

He felt his throat constrict.

Artuah had not known the full intentions of Father or of the Plan laid down by *Abba Father Himself* but it had been passed along to them all by the Ancient. He had received it directly from the Beyond. Had received it! In Vision! In Dream!

Flood.

Ham shivered when he thought of this word. He knew that the River swelled in its Season and that sometimes the Rain came and made it so also. But this! From what the Ancient had conveyed to him, or had tried to, he could not grasp it. He had spoken about the Plain and the Valley turning into the 'Sea.' He had heard about the Sea and knew that it was Water so vast that you could not see to its opposite bank but he had never before seen it for himself. It was said that once Seth, the Great Father, had lived near to a Great River in a place called 'Beginning' and that it was as vast as the Sea but he could not imagine such a thing. And why was such great Water a part of *Abba Father's* Plan anyway?

It made no sense. None of it. Visions. Dreams! Surely one day he would experience such wonders? Looking back, he caught sight of the Ancient again, striding along, gripping his javelin in his gnarled hand. The old man had indeed insisted on coming as well and would not be dissuaded. He had still a Task to be done, he had said, just like his grandson now had. This he said he knew. It was an absolute Truth. Only he did not know exactly what it was yet.

Ham shook his head. It was ironic. The Ancient knew of Flood, knew of the Fate of the Family, of the Fate of the World, and yet did not know his own.

"It is Faith," Ham burst out, suddenly, with new understanding and walking the River Path for perhaps the last time. And he felt his heart throbbing with conviction. "That is all that he has now, all that he has to go on. All that we all have to go on! All that we can know now is within our hearts."

Mother looked over at him again. "Ah," she said, nodding toward him. "I see that my Prayers are being heard at last, My Son. You are learning."

He beamed.

Overhead, the River-birds circled and cried and off toward the Eastern rise of the Valley, he could hear the tracks of many smaller Animals following along beside them.

They too are accompanying us. But where do we all go?

Into Abba Father's arms?

Into Faith?

Into Flood.

XIV

Righteous in this generation. That is what He called me. Yet have I now failed Him?

He sat huddled in the doorway of the cave, staring out toward the gap in the Mountains, his staff laid across his lap.

The River had cut off the fording place, the access to the Ark.

And the rest of the Family had not come.

"I was too late in sending him. My beloved servant and friend," he groaned into the teeth of the wind that came from the Mountains. He could feel it whipping his hair and even his long, white beard. His robe fluttered out behind him, snapping, and his face was slick with stinging rain. It had finally begun in earnest and overhead the black sky churned with ominous clouds.

"How can we board the Ark, *Abba Father*?" he whispered, "How can we board the Ark without *them?*"

He felt lost. And though he would never admit it to any other living soul, he was also afraid. *Abba Father, what am I to do? Show me!*

And suddenly he was thinking of the Animals. He did not know why. They had come in time, hadn't they? All of those which *Abba Father* had called clean - seven pairs each of the Ox, the Deer, the Gazelle, the Ibex, the Antelope. They had all come from different directions from the Mountains and were even now within the Ark. They had come earlier, before the River had surged angrily in its banks and many more had done so besides. As well did those come which He had called unclean, two pairs of each - the Camel, the Rabbit, the Pig among them. They had all come in lesser numbers, it was True, but they had come also, each finding their own way to the Valley, to the Ark. And there had been the Birds of the air too. The Eagle, the Ibis, the Vulture, the Kite, the Falcon, the Raven, the Owl, the Osprey, the Cormorant, the Stork, the Heron, and even the Bat. They had filled the skies with their coming! Many others there were as well and he could not even name them all!

All had come and had entered the Ark before the Rain had begun and the River had risen and there they were still. Waiting for the End.

Except for the Rams. That thought also crashed through his mind. *They are still here on this side with the rest of us - so Shem tells it. They have left their ewes and refused absolutely all chances to go in! Again, so he tells it.*

Noah sighed.

Now it was all for nothing. It was too late. All of them were lost.

"The Flood will come and carry us all away."

"Father!"

He jerked and then lurched unsteadily to his feet, gripping his long stick painfully in his hand. The wind tore at his robe and he swept a hand savagely over his hair to keep it out of his eyes.

Shem was stepping quickly along the River's edge below him.

Aha! The tale-teller, himself.

He watched as his son moved toward the path of flat stones that led up to the cave's maw. "Father," he called up, "You must come to the Verge right away! Japheth says that - !" - but then the wind rose up in a fury and whipped the rest of his words away into the air.

Noah cupped a hand to his ear and shook his head. Shen climbed the path and reached out to clutch his elbow. His eyes were wide and round and the old man could see their whites in the misty spray all around them. He bent his mouth to Noah's ear.

"It's the Rams!" he shouted above the wind. "Like I told you before. It seems *Abba Father* has…..commanded them to do something. Something! I don't know what!"

"Commanded?!" Noah yelled back at him, thinking he had misheard.

"Yes!" answered Shem, quickly. "They are standing at the Verge and will not be moved for anything or anyone!"

Noah drew away, frowning. "What does it mean?" he called out. "Has the Family arrived yet?"

Shem shook his head impatiently. "Just come!" he shouted and he beckoned wildly.

Noah took his stick in hand and followed after his son. They did not stop until they reached the Verge.

"Straight ahead, Daughter! That is what he said. Do not falter, do not stop! We must arrive in time! *He* will watch over us!"

"So you say, Ancient," grimaced Emzara in the face of the rain and of the bitter wind. "So you have said this entire journey."

Ham came and stood beside her. Wordlessly, he slipped his arm through hers and together they forged ahead, walking through the tall grass near the surging river away on their left, faces held down against the fury of the wind and the rain.

'We couldn't see Father and my brothers in this if we tripped over them!' he thought, dismally.

Turning his head, he looked over at the river beside them for the hundredth time. He could not lose his awe of it. Nor did he want to. It was *the* River! This he knew deep down in his very bones. They *had* to be going the right way. This too, he had told himself for the hundredth time. Surely, *Abba Father* would see them to the others safely? Surely He would save them from this wind and rain; from this Flood?

"I need only Trust in Him," he murmured to himself beneath the howl of the wind. "Only Trust."

Mother looked at him through the beating, relentless rain and he saw that she, too, knew that they were going now on Faith alone. There was nothing left. It was all behind them now. Forever.

"I will hasten back to Artuah!" shouted the old man, from behind them again. Ham gave a start and turned to see the Ancient lifting his javelin and pointing it back along the way they had come. He had almost forgotten about the old man. And beside him, he caught sight of his good-sisters. He was suddenly aware that his wife stood with them.

"Neltamuk!" he cried out and she came to him, smiling forlornly in the wet. Quickly, emphatically, they embraced.

"My parents say that they will stand now with the Archer and the Ancient," she said, drawing away from him, "and that I should now stand with my husband - even if he be yet only my Intended."

Ham reached out and grasped the wet sleeve of her cloak. "And he shall stand with his wife," he said.

"So should it be," said Mother, watching and nodding.

In that very instant, the end came at last.

Oh, it was not yet the End of all things but only the end of their journey within the high valley. For suddenly Ham looked up and saw the mist seem to roll back before his eyes. "What's that?" he cried out. "Ahead? Are they torches?"

And then from the rear, slicing through the rain at the same instant, came Artuah's piercing shout: "Behind us! They have found us at last!"

Curse this Rain! Curse this Valley! Curse this Wind! If I have to trudge ten more steps in all of this with no result I will slice open that Sethite's throat myself and have done with it!

He had had to abandon his chariot at the Water-Fall even though he could have passed it through. Once faced with the stony valley between the cliffs and the thick grass, however, it was impossible to proceed with it and so he had bowed, ungraciously, to necessity. It had put him in the midst of, and on the same level as, his men and he preferred to be above them. How could they look up to him and serve him if they did not have to lift up their eyes to behold him? He was their Lord and Master and it was his will that drove them - and his will that would reward them when they had accomplished their goals. Those goals which he had set for them. And so here he trudged through the wet grass and driving wind and rain, no higher or better than they. A faceless slave!

What was worse was that he was utterly dwarfed now by the two *Eneph* who had come with them and who had pledged to him their great spears. Even now they were flanking him and his armour-bearer and the Sethite like two vast shadows of death, hidden partly by the mist and rain but still unmistakable, enormous presences - like twin shadows of foreboding.

Perhaps I should not have accepted their pledge. Perhaps I should have left them behind even if they did not want to heed their Seer.

But he knew deep in his guts that they would never have stayed behind.

They want to kill that improbable man, that Ancient. That's what they said. But why didn't they kill him when they had the chance? Did something stop them? He couldn't imagine anything that could. *I told them to do it! The Seer pledged that they would!*

He did not understand it. "I will have to finish the job yet on my own," he growled beneath the wind and the rain. "But they can have the Ancient. He is no longer of any account. Not now. It's *him* that I want. The one who sets himself up as the Lord of Seth."

Soon, all that would be left of that House; of that miserable brother of Cain would be death and not even a memory.

Grimly, he continued on through the deluge.

A-Phthah felt himself wilt as he walked with the one who had once been Elah-Makah but who now called himself 'Lord of Men.' He felt his age as he had never before felt it; felt his body begin to reach its limit.

And now here I stand shoulder to shoulder with him! At the End! A shame! A dishonour! A Traitor to all that is Good!

His back ached and his arms ached and his legs ached. Everywhere was pain. But mostly he felt it in his soul.

Ah, Abba Father, can you forgive me? Can You ever forgive a wretch of a man who has betrayed his Master and all Good people on this failing Earth?

He looked toward the sound of the River, which had been a constant guide above the din of the rain and the moaning of the wind for so long now. It was the path toward the Master and yet also the mark of his own treachery!

He gasped. Then he frowned.

Abba Father? Are You speaking?

Then he knew.

He had been meant to be here! Now! This moment! He had been meant to bring *him* here! He glanced sidelong at Lamech beside him. It was not Treachery at all, what he had done. It was Destiny. Both his and his Enemy's.

In that instant of seeing and knowing, he froze. "There they are!" he shouted, suddenly, raising his arm and pointing it straight ahead into the rolling mist.

Ahead was only a faceless, grey curtain.

"HALT!" screamed Lamech then and everything and everyone stopped. The King squinted into the driving rain and wind and his outer cloak snapped behind him. He turned and bore his dark eyes upon

A-Phthah. "You had better be right about this, Sethite," he growled, "I had better see damnable Sethites in front of me or I'll slit - "

"Look!" shouted a voice then and A-Phthah knew it to be the King's chief soldier, the general Dalkus. "Forms through the mist!"

And there, to the servant of Seth's wonder, ghostly figures of men suddenly appeared, emerging from the fog, not fifty paces ahead! Somehow, they were there. Somehow they could be seen. Perhaps the rain was relenting. Perhaps the mist was withdrawing.

Perhaps they were even real.

It is a miracle. "A trap?" A-Phthah whispered, and he felt his heart pounding deep within him. "Is it a trap that you have set, *Abba Father?*"

Lamech snapped his head around and looked straight at him again, a terrible scowl twisting his dark lips.

"Dalkus!" he shouted, black eyes still locked upon A-Phthah, "Sound the horn! We shall spread out and face them! Draw swords! If it's a last stand that he wants, we shall oblige him!"

Abruptly, the cry of the horn by the heralds of the Army burst forth into the soupy greyness, slicing through the wet and wind and mist, and in the midst of that high valley its echoes were terrifying. The sound of the soldiers drawing their blades came immediately afterward and A-Phthah heard it as the sound of Doom. Nearby, he saw the two *Eneph* take up their giant spears, clutching them tightly in both hands.

"Now watch, Sethite," Lamech growled at him, putting on his helm and summoning his armour-bearer. "Watch as your master and all that is left of his House dies."

The ancient grain fields lay sodden and inundated. He could see sullen, grey pools here and there where the water no longer ran off toward the river. Indeed, the river itself, rushing by on their right, threatened to overrun its banks at any moment.

"Father," said a grey shadow as it emerged from the general greyness of the dying, old world. It was Japheth. "We don't have much time." He shot an arm up and pointed toward the bushes that had emerged from the shadows behind him.

Noah could see the outline of them. He squinted.

"Is that the Animals?" he asked, pointing his own crooked finger ahead. "Standing in front of them? The rams?"

Blurs of lighter grey seemed to cluster at the feet of the Verge.

"Indeed," said Japheth, passing a soaking sleeve of his cloak over his face. His skin had almost become leeched of all colour in the ceaseless rain, his father noticed. "Eight of them, to be exact. And I'm sure you won't hold with this but I do believe they are waiting for you."

"And what is that?" cried the old man, suddenly, pointing along the valley toward the East.

Startled, Japheth whirled and Shem came, hastily, to stand with them. Together, the three of them gaped in silence.

Beyond the Verge, *hovering* in the air in the midst of the rain, were two great…..objects. They were throbbing and pulsing with a suffused light and rippling in the very air, like gently stirring waters on the surface of a flowing river! Noah was speechless, throat working noiselessly, as he watched them.

Shem let out a long, almost hissing, breath that rose above the susurration of the rain and Noah could see his eyes as wide as copper plates. "By *Abba Father, Himself!*" he breathed. "They are insects! Insects of light!"

"Shem. Japheth." Noah spoke in a daze. "Go and see what approaches along the valley. It is a Sign from our God and Protector. Go!"

Beside him, his sons jumped. Wordlessly, they headed off into the rain toward the undulating globs of light.

"And me?" whispered Noah into the wind. He forced his eyes from the direction of his disappearing sons and turned them once more upon the Verge. He trembled. There was another Sign that he must heed and he must do so *now!*

Japtheth and the pasture-lad had told him about the earlier peculiar behaviour of the mules near the Verge. Japtheth had shown him the bare area of rock within it, near its tip. The moment he had first seen it, he could admit now, had meant nothing to him. He did not understand it. Any of it. What it was. What purpose it served. Only that it served one - as yet unattained.

He thought he saw that purpose now. Standing here in this place with the eight Animals around him, around it, waiting, he glimpsed it at last.

Upon the edge of the bare space, half-buried in the roots and scarce, all-but washed away soil of the bushes, was a knife of stone.

He reached and took up the ancient blade - for of this there was no doubt; it was more ancient than anything that he had ever before seen - and as he did so he saw it upraised toward a crimson sky in the hand of another, gone long before. The vision catapulted itself into his mind, making him shudder with its visceral clarity. It was a young hand, a very young hand, and it had held this blade under a dawn sky the colour of blood.

"Ah, *Abba Father,*" he croaked, for he saw now what God had set for him.

The rain beat down and lightning and thunder flashed and rolled around him. He clutched the knife and turned to the first Animal that stood, docilely, at his elbow. It did not utter a sound but merely looked at him with unblinking eyes. With his free hand, he caught it around the throat. It did not resist.

Bracing himself, he pronounced over it, "Noah, the son of Lamech of Seth, the son of Methuselah," and the knife moved in his hand.

The rain mingled with the offering of life-blood upon the rock.

Likewise, did Noah offer up the life of each of the other seven rams, naming them in turn. His trembling lips, slick with the rain, spoke each one:

"Emzara."

"Shem."

"Japheth."

"Ham."

"Sedeqe."

"Hadata."

And.....

And?

"Neltamuk," he whispered.

He did not know who that was. But he knew that he would know her very soon.

Eight lives. Eight lives were to be purchased. Eight lives were to be held back from the Doom of the Fallen World.

As soon as the last name had escaped Noah's lips, a brilliant flash of light filled all the world and a searing wall of heat threw him back into the scraggly, wet bushes all around him! He lay dazed and insensible and -

And quite blind.

"Father! Father!" came Japheth's voice from the blackness. "Are you all right? We saw the lightning! We could *feel* it in the air!"

Yes, I know. It almost had me!

"And the Family! The Family! They followed the lights! It was a beacon for them to find! They're here! Shem is leading them to the fording place even now! The River! The *River! The wind has thrown it back at just that spot! We can cross!*"

"*Abba Father*, be praised!" Noah croaked and his hands shot out to search for his staff. "Quick!" He found it where he had lain it down along the thin path in the Verge. He grasped it and lifted it high. "Here!" he cried. "I am here! We must go to join them. There is not a moment to lose!"

Soon the wet sound of the bushes being thrust aside along the narrow path came to him.

"Father!" came Japtheth's voice nearby. "What are you doing?"

Noah raised his other hand. "No matter! Help me up. Guide me."

"Guide you?" repeated Shem, confused.

"I cannot see from God's fire," he shouted.

At once, he felt the other take his hand and pull him up onto his feet. He clutched at Shem's sleeve.

"It is finished," he told him. "Now to the Ark! And new Life!"

"There!" said Methuselah, pointing at the floating clouds of light. He accepted them as a decree from *Abba Father, Himself.* There was no other way to accept them or to believe that they were real. "Go! Now! Not a second can you lose! It comes now swiftly! Leave the supplies!"

Then Emzara took up the cry: "Let us go to meet with Father and your Brothers, My Son and My Daughters! Quickly now!"

At once, the five of the Family that had journeyed into the high valley so lately moved on ahead into the mist and the old man with his javelin and Artuah, who had come to stand with him now, bow at the ready, watched them depart.

At the very fringe of the curtain of fog, one of the Five paused and looked back. The old man could see the warmth and care in her eyes, even from where he stood.

"Go, My Child!" he croaked out. "Go and see the New World that He has prepared for you! Go in Peace."

Neltamuk smiled, sadly, at him and then turned back and disappeared into the fog with her husband.

"Ancient!" screamed Artuah behind him, then, "The Enemy is upon us!"

He whirled, his javelin raised high in his hand.

"Dalkus! Attack! Keep the Lord of Seth for me!"

"We seek the Ancient!" bellowed the *Eneph,* as the soldiers of Cain surged forward. With a cry, they raged against the line of men in the fog and rain and lightning and thunder.

Lamech ran forward, his sword uplifted, eyes searching feverishly through the gloom for his Adversary. *You cannot escape the might and Fate of Cain, Upstart!*

He stood in the midst of the line of now thrashing, grappling bodies. The Enemy were a ragged, soaking, miserable bunch. He saw it at once. Slaves. No more. No doubt, *he* would call them servants. There were none of the Family. None of the direct line of that most hated of Blood. And yet these slaves fought with a gleam of something in their eyes, didn't they? He could, at first, not understand it. He brought his heavy blade down upon two of them, cutting them down, sending them back to the earth from which they had come and still they fought. Others surged through the mist, carrying implements and tools, brandishing them over their heads, crying out in loud voices as if they tried to beseech the All-Father to see their bravery.

They do not fight for themselves.

The thought came slowly into his mind as he flashed his blade and struck at them without mercy. *They fight for something else. SomeONE else.*

"Find him!" he screamed, then, through the fog. "Find him now! I need to kill him before it's too late! Before they have too much hope!"

Then, ahead, a man with a bow emerged from the fog not twenty paces ahead of him. He paused a moment to look at him. *Not HIM but not a mere servant this time either.* He could see it right away. This one was a soldier.

"Come on, then!" the King screamed but, in a flash, an arrow was nocked to the Sethite soldier's bow and its stone tip was pointed straight at his face.

He had time only to gasp before the Sethite loosed his arrow. In the instant it left the bow, however, a giant spear of an *Eneph* pierced him straight through the chest and he fell to the flooded grass without a sound.

The Sethite's arrow struck Lamech of Cain in the left shoulder, between the joints of his bronze-clad armour.

He cried out in pain, clutching at his arm, and quickly pulled the arrow free. He could feel blood flowing freely and warmly down his arm. At once, Dalkus was there. "No sign, My King!" he shouted above the torrent, clutching Lamech with his free hand and helping to steady him. "No sign of the Lord of Seth whom you seek!"

One of the *Eneph* appeared out of the gloom, then, and placed his great, bronze-shod boot upon the fallen Sethite archer. He pulled the huge spear from the lifeless body. "Not for you, Lord of Men," he growled at Lamech, and the King could see that his liquid, green eyes seemed dulled by the relentless rain, as if they had been leached of their light, as if they fought to stay alit, "but only for the greatness of my Brethren."

"Brother!" shouted the other in a tremendous roar over the thunder, emerging from the rolling mist. This one's eyes, saw Lamech, were a pale blue. *"He* is here! I saw him in the flash of lightning! Come!"

Together, the two monsters stalked off into the dimness. Dalkus went off after them and disappeared, leaving him standing alone within the maelstrom. The battle seemed to have moved on.

Suddenly, he started. He staggered on his feet, his arm a blazing furnace of pain.

"I am not where they seek me," said a voice over the tumult. "For *Abba Father* has hidden me from their sight."

The Lord of Cain stood staring at the old man and he felt himself tremble.

"I am the King," Lamech croaked out, but his sword in his sword-hand hung limply at his side. It felt as heavy as a chariot.

"You are the King," the old man agreed, nodding in the blinding sheets of rain that came down between them from the unseen Heavens. "The King of the Lost Souls. The King of the Fallen World."

A fire kindled in Lamech's chest then.

"I once had a son named Lamech," spoke the old man, then, louder, and he held his javelin loosely in his gnarled hand. "Did you know that? He was a righteous man. You would not know him. Fitting, don't you think?"

The fire began to spread through Lamech's body and it was as if the Great Father, himself, were kindling it, giving a portion of the strength of the last of the Line of Cain to him for just this moment. Perhaps, it was power even from the All-Father! His Enemy saw it, for the old man's eyes grew wide.

Lamech shouted out in defiance of Seth, of Noah, of Methuselah, the Ancient, and even in defiance of the One they called *Abba Father!*

But it was not enough.

The javelin rose and sailed through the air but it was not thrown by that ancient, gnarled hand alone. The Hand that hurled it did so with such force that the rain did not touch it and it buried itself deep within Lamech's chest, slicing clear through his armour.

With a ghastly choke, the King fell to his knees. Methuselah heard his throat gurgling and saw his eyes glaze over and raise up toward the lost sky. Slowly, the head lowered to the broken chest and the shaft protruding from it and there the King of the Fallen world remained as the rain fell and the lightning flashed and the thunder rolled.

Methuselah looked upon Lamech for a moment before the ground shook and moved beneath his very feet. A great chasm was rent open in the very Earth and the ancient, inundated grainfield began to slide down into it. Even as it did so, however, water came spewing violently UP from the yawning fissure.

Abba Father, take me!

And He did.

A-Phthah lost track of the battle in the fog. He had no weapon in any case. It was not why he had been brought here by *Abba Father's* mighty hand. His task had been only to point the way toward the line of men standing before them in the mist, just as he had pointed the way for the entire journey since the Palace, what seemed like days ago. *There is nothing else for me to do. I had to bring him and I have.*

He caught a glimpse of something through the fog and he jerked his head up toward it. The two *Eneph* emerged before him, spears held up at the ready.

"It is not him!" screamed the one with the dulled-blue eyes, seeing him. The green-eyed one gave a snarl of rage and then, suddenly, incomprehensibly, they turned on one another, tearing and ripping at each other with their bare hands and teeth! Growling and snarling, they fought and A-Phthah, speechless, watched them.

They have become like Animals! It is the Judgement of Abba Father!

Then the ground shook violently and he felt it give way beneath his feet.

Together with his fearsome enemies, he slid down into the Earth.

But felt the Hand of God wrap around him and take him to another place, a place of warmth and light.

And no more Pain.

They passed quickly on and left the fording place behind, the river held up as if by giant, unseen Hands, and made their way, the eight of them to the Ark. They did not speak. Noah walked last, his sight now restored and his arms and his staff upraised behind his family. It was as if he were trying to shield them from the fury and righteous wrath of God that churned about them.

Abba Father, a little farther! A little farther and we are there. Within your bosom. Within the shelter of your wings.

Emzara led them, still clutching Ham's hand within hers. His was clutched in Neltamuk's. The rest of the brothers and their wives came after, directly in front of Noah.

"The Ark!" shouted Emzara, seeing its huge bulk loom out of the dimness, and she had not even a moment to marvel at it. For her, it simply was and that was enough. She stepped upon its great ramp and then moved aside, beckoning and thrusting the Family up past her. "Quickly!"

And now the ground was shaking beneath their feet and beneath the behemoth of wood.

Noah stomped onto the ramp and then clutched his wife and together they thrust themselves up after the others.

They huddled together within the confines of the giant vessel of Hope that had sprung from the mind of God.

It was dark where they were, with the rage of the dying world outside and all around them but there was an awesome presence of others with them. The Animals. Noah felt them everywhere. They were silent beneath the fury of God outside of the Ark but they were there.

Then Japheth shouted out, "The doorway - !"

But the giant ramp had already lifted itself up, raising itself as if within the very Hand of God, Himself - or was it only the wind? In the heart and mind of each of them, they knew the answer.

It was God, Himself, therefore, Who shut them in.

They felt the Ark lifted up and set upon the surging Waters outside.

In the darkness, as the great vessel moved and groaned beneath and around them, they began to sing a hymn that the Great Father Seth, himself, had composed and which they had not sung in a long, long time.

XV

Kalneh, the Great City, had shut itself up. In the midst of the storm, Ohun, the Head Chamberlain of the Palace, had sent out the Patrols of the Recruits into its districts. In the Name of the King, he was imposing a curfew of her citizens until such time as the King should return. It was Lamech's standing order in the event of inclement weather in time of war in order to secure the sacred boundary of the City from possible enemy ambush or domestic treachery.

The weather had also delayed the Offering atop the Ziggurat.

It was the morning of the second full day since the King's departure, and Ohun had convened with the Queens within the Council Chamber, just off of the Main Chamber. The Heavenly Lights did not look down upon them here but perhaps it made no difference as the fog and the rain outside had all but obscured them in the real, lost skies above the City. In a great number of places within the Palace, the wind could be heard moaning and wailing like a living creature. Many of the servants had come to him, badly frightened, but he had had no time for them today. Today could not be wasted on the likes of them.

"My Queens," he intoned, spreading his arms wide over the Council Table, his fingers splayed. "I enjoin you before the Great Father and the All-Father, to consider the Sacred Rite. His Majesty, the King, is at War and it has not been performed."

"And the King has not returned," Adah murmured.

Where is he? Where is my husband? Has the Great Father not bestowed upon him the strength of Cain? Or has he stripped it away? Has the All-Father prepared for him a great Test which he will fail? She had tied her long, black hair in the twin braids, bound together tightly behind the neck and had rubbed the *akhulah* upon her lips and below her eyes as well as above them so that any, she knew, who looked upon them while they were closed would see only open, black pits sinking down into Nothingness.

She had sworn the *hol-nah*. The Death Pledge.

She had known it was time. Oh, yes. When the rain had not abated but had only increased and the wind had grown to a howl, she knew that what she had vowed to do could be put off no longer. Last night, in the dark of her apartments, by only the light of a single tallow candle held by the hand of her precious Li-et, she had sworn that terrible oath to the Spirits of air, earth, and below the earth. If her vow was not done this day, she would take her own life by her own hand with the sacred blade and let the All-Father and the spirits have her.

Ohun cleared his throat. "The Sacred Rite of Propitiation must be offered. The Laws of the Kingdom are clear: storm or no storm, it must be offered by the second full day. Today. Now. At Sunrise."

As if in answer, a crash of thunder shook the Chamber walls and even set a tapestry of the Great City hanging over the near one to swaying.

The Chamberlain swallowed. This morning there had been no Sunrise as he and all within the Palace well knew. He turned to one of his Mistresses, the one who sat upon his right. "As senior Queen, Adah of the East," he began, "it is your right - "

"I waive my right," interjected Adah, cutting him off, and Ohun found himself staring once more into those dark pits within her face. A cold sweat broke out on his brow. Adah turned toward his other Mistress, who sat upon his left. "I bestow my right of First Offering to my Sister Queen. Zillah." He saw the lips, as black as night, twist upward at one corner. "The North shall have the Honour, for this storm comes from both West and North. The East, in this matter, shall be the follower."

He saw the pale, grey Northern eyes turn toward the Eastern dark circles.

"The Honour, Sister Queen," whispered Zillah to Adah, "I accept."

Ohun sighed, a great, long sigh, and sat back in his chair. Whatever had happened, whatever had just passed, it would take its course. The lightning flashed and the thunder shook the Palace.

There were but few Recruits who could be spared to escort the Queens to the Ziggurat. Adah walked beside her Rival across the rain-drenched, dismal Plaza of the Sun and ahead of them and behind were two pairs of

Recruits. She could see that they were but boys, barely old enough to pass the razor over their cheeks. Smiling to herself despite the solemnity of the moment and the sacred hour, she knew that her husband would call them, 'Green.' And she doubted that anything that was left in all the world was green any longer. All colour had been leached away. All beaten down and carried away by the deluge. Indeed, their escort struggled in vain to keep the awning over their heads. It was all but useless, for there was no way of keeping the wind and the rain from them.

In truth, she no longer cared. Not for propriety, not for the Sacred Rite, not for anything. There was only one thing left for which she cared. She raised her eyes to the Ziggurat looming over them as they reached the end of the Plaza. She could feel the *akhulah* running down her cheeks, washing away in the torrent.

Suddenly, a small hand gripped hers. She jumped and her heart leapt within her for she knew that something must be happening in the Spirit World. It was close now. Very close. She did not look down at the owner of that hand.

"Mistress," Li-et hissed into the wind. "He is dead."

Her hand gripped the smaller one back. She heard the words but did not reply. A trembling seized her.

"I feel it," the voice went on in the storm and it seemed to her to be drenched in pain. Or was it ecstasy? "I see it in the Darkness. The King is dead."

Ahead, the foremost pair of escorts halted at the foot of the grand staircase of the Ziggurat. After a moment's hesitation, she watched her rival begin to ascend it alone.

Adah drew back, breathing rapidly, hand still clutching the waif's desperately in her own.

He is dead! The All-Father has prepared this moment. He has prepared it for me! No husband. Soon no rival. No other.

Her hand was shaking violently now as she watched the other climb the stone steps. "Oh, My Pet," she breathed in the falling rain. "My Pet!"

And the small hand slipped free from hers.

"The King is dead!" she screamed when they were gone, the both of them.

She turned to the terrified Recruits and raised her arms at them.

"Go tell Ohun that there is a new Prince in this City and in this Kingdom. Even in all the world!" She hurled the words at them as if they were weapons. "And she is coming in wrath!"

The awning blew away across the Plaza and the raw soldiers fled from her, boots splashing through the water. The Plaza was awash now. Rivers were flowing into it from all of the streets of the City and the rain began to fall in sheets. Lightning seared the skies and thunder clove the air. For a brief moment, she faced the stair and tilted her head to the skies and let the water slide down her face, down her neck, into her robes. She felt it slick her entire body.

Then she began to climb.

Zillah gained the top of the stairs at last and set her foot upon the Apex of the Ziggurat. In her hands was the flask of Offering - the mixed blood of all of the remaining prisoners within the dungeons. They had been hastily slain last night when the King had still not returned, their blood now the Sin Offering of Kalneh and the Propitiation of the All-Father.

Slowly, she turned toward the Image upon its pedestal. She raised her eyes toward its face.

"My Queen," came a voice behind her, and it was like a ghastly croak. She stopped and looked back.

A small figure in a hooded cloak knelt upon the last step of the grand staircase. In its small hands was a box of ivory.

"My Mistress wishes to expiate her own sin," croaked the voice again, "before you offer the expiation of the whole Kingdom. It is only right."

"You are Adah's creature," said Zillah, numbly, in the rain. "What are you doing here?" She looked down upon the girl with revulsion.

"My Mistress has wronged the Queen of the North. The Spirits have seen it. The Spirits bear witness to it. In humble contrition, therefore, My Mistress begs the Queen for her forgiveness." The girl opened the box and lifted it in her hands. "She sends a token." The croaking voice emanating from the hood had become no more than a hiss now. It was barely audible over the wind and the rain.

Zillah's eyes strayed to the box.

Inside, the Queen's eyes caught a glimpse of gold. Even in the ceaseless rain, it seemed to glint up at her and to beckon to her.

Open-mouthed, she moved toward it. The girl held the box up high in her hands but it was still too low to reach.

Zillah bent down and took the ring in her right hand.

There was a movement, a flicker, at the corner of her eye, and she looked down upon the ring sitting in her open hand. Confused, she saw that it was not gold but red. She looked at her palm and it too was red. Her head began to swim and she felt her legs buckle beneath her. The stone platform at the very top of the world rushed up at her and she found herself looking up at a small shadow standing over her in the rain. It held a tiny blade covered in blood in its hand.

Adah reached the top of the stairs just as Li-et returned the small knife to the folds of her cloak. There, upon the stone, lay her Rival. She could see the tangle of wet, royal robes and the river of red flowing from the open throat and down the stairs, could see the rain falling upon the open, staring, grey eyes. She knelt down in the wet beside the unmoving body, her own robes sodden. She lowered her face over the dead woman's and laid her hand upon the now-stilled heart.

"Now see your True Queen, *Your Majesty.*" Her mouth twisted at one end at these words and she felt the water dripping from her lips.

Slowly, she reached over to pry the flask from the curling, dead fingers. Then she rose to her feet and turned toward the huge Image of the black Serpent.

"All-Father!" she cried into the storm. "Behold me! Behold the True Queen and Ruler of this Wor - "

But the Ziggurat shook on its very foundation and sent her sprawling to the stone platform.

"Mistress!" screamed Li-et, and never before had Adah heard her utter such a sound.

Adah regained her knees but no more, for she looked up and saw, far out beyond the City, over the Plain, the distant cliff-face of the Mountains in the West collapse in a vast tumult of rock and earth and seething water. Before her very eyes, the Plain itself began to split apart and crumble away. Geysers of water shot up in steaming bursts, each as big as a Town. The Plain heaved and broke apart. Her throat worked as she watched but no sound came.

Now the ground beneath the City was shaking violently. She could feel the Ziggurat groan and sway beneath her. The staircase cracked in two from its base to its pinnacle and began to split apart. At the top of the stairs, Li-et and the dead woman fell into the chasm and were gone without a sound. Beside her, the Image of the All-father itself groaned upon its plinth and began to slowly lower toward the abyss as if in silent supplication. She saw its red eyes dulled and quenched and dead. It too slid into the fissure and was gone.

And now finally the stone beneath her was giving way. She felt it shift and move and, silently, she looked down into a chasm, a rent, opening and yawning into the very Earth itself right at her knees. For a brief moment, she felt a shimmering heat touch her cheeks.

Adah, the Queen, saw that in this abyss, her very own, there was no water. Only fire.

EPILOGUE

The three of them climbed to the Upper Deck with great care, Shem flinging open the trap before them. Ham, in the rear, felt his boot slip upon the last rung as he gained the deck after his brothers and then he stooped and re-shut the trap. As always the Birds were constant companions up here, mostly the Shore and Water Birds. Father had opened the windows and he saw several of them *outside* the Ark even now, flying just above the surface of the Water, which Father had called the Sea, crying and calling, as if playing with the wooden behemoth that cleaved the endless waters. Amongst these especially did he spy the Albatrosses. Ah, they could fly great distances over the flooded Earth and always return just when you thought they had perished from it! Ham had actually befriended one soon after God had shut them all in and had watched it fly off at least twice since then for weeks at a time! Others there were who roosted within the open, wooden sills. Some of the tiny Sparrows and Swallows could be spotted up here as well and today he tried greeting them gently but they ignored his voice, preferring to roost instead.

Beneath them, the floor gently rose and fell and the great, pitched walls of cypress groaned on either side. This effect was greatest up here on the Upper Deck, Ham had quickly discovered. He had climbed to this place many times now since the Ark had first been raised up on the surge and had left the high valley and even the mountains behind all those days ago. Today, however, the Sea was quieter and the wind had fallen off. Even the thick cover of dark clouds had begun to slowly lighten and to break up in the sky revealing its old, soft blue colour.

"He's for'ard," called Shem to them and the three started carefully ahead.

'Father has measured it as nigh on to five months since we have entered the Ark,' thought Ham. *'He says he has been watching the Lights at night since the Rain stopped and every now and then he can spot them in the night sky through the clouds. So he has figured it out. But I cannot believe it. It feels more like five years than five months! Where is the Valley of Seth now, I wonder? Does it still exist or has it been changed forever, washed away?*' He liked to think that it was always near somehow and that when the Water finally receded it would be there just waiting for them to reclaim it as their Home. But Father did not hold to this view. He said that everything that once was would be gone and that all the world would be New. They would need to start over again. The Family. The eight of them. They would be all that was left of the Peoples who had been.

Ham shivered even though the breeze was light and almost warm as he thought about this. They would need to build a whole new world! He thought of Neltamuk and of the new life inside her. A symbol of the New Beginning itself.

"Father!" called Shem as they approached the bow. Noah stood at the very front of the Ark, peering out through the high window that he had had put here for just such a purpose. "To see where *Abba Father* pulls us," he had told them once, the twinkle having returned to his light-brown eyes. The night of the beginning of the Flood when the Family had been finally reunited and the servants had fought Lamech had taken a severe toll on Father. Ham could see it. He had only slowly regained his good health and good nature through the worst of the great Storm but once the Rain had finally stopped, he had recovered more quickly and they were all glad to see it.

"Ah!" said Father and he embraced each of them. He lingered last over Ham and whispered in his ear, "I hear that the honeymoon at Sea has been a great success." Ham reddened and Noah chuckled.

Shem was looking through the window now at the gently swelling, blue-green horizon. "How far does the World go, Father?" he asked, quietly and they all became still then, looking out ahead at the rolling Water.

"Ah," sighed Father. "Only *HE* knows the Truth of that."

They gasped.

The clouds had broken up enough for a ray of light from the sun to stab down from the sky! A single ray. And it brought more than just light for behold! a marvellous band of radiant colours shone down to the surface of the Sea beneath it! It seemed to stretch from the sky to touch the Water before them, dazzling their eyes!

Suddenly, they heard a Voice in the sighing of the wind and even the Birds fell silent:

"I have set my rainbow in the clouds and it will be the sign of the covenant between Me and the Earth. Whenever I bring clouds over the Earth and the rainbow appears in the clouds I will see it and I will remember. Never again will I destroy all living creatures. As long as the Earth endures, seedtime and harvest, cold and heat, summer and winter, day and night will never cease."

"Amen," said Noah and his three sons stood behind him. He raised his hand and in it was a dove.

"Go," said Noah to the bird. "Find our new world."

And with Hope in their hearts, they watched it take wing over the Water.